JOHN TREEGATE'S MUSKET

Also by Leonard Wibberley

FOR YOUNG PEOPLE:

The Treegate Series:

Peter Treegate's War
Sea Captain from Salem
Treegate's Raiders
Leopard's Prey
Red Pawns
The Last Battle

•

Flint's Island

•

Man of Liberty:
A Life of Thomas Jefferson

•

The Life of Winston Churchill

FOR ADULTS:

The Hands of Cormac Joyce
Stranger at Killknock
The Mouse That Roared
The Last Stand of Father Felix

John Treegate's Musket

Leonard Wibberley

with an Afterword by the author

BETHLEHEM BOOKS • IGNATIUS PRESS
Bathgate   San Francisco

First Bethlehem Books printing September 2007

ISBN 978-1-932350-16-6
Library of Congress Control Number: 2007928551

Bethlehem Books • Ignatius Press
10194 Garfield Street South
Bathgate, North Dakota 58216
www.bethlehembooks.com
1-800-757-6831

Printed in the United States on acid-free paper

JOHN TREEGATE'S MUSKET

Chapter 1

THE YEAR was 1769 and the place Boston—Boston, a city of seamen and of merchants, of importers and exporters, of shopkeepers and manufacturers, of prosperous bankers and ragged ne'er-do-wells, of gentlemen dressed in the latest London fashion, and others dressed in the clothing home-designed of materials which were home-woven.

In the streets of this Boston were gentlemen whose wigs were made in England and powdered with chalk from France, and others whose hair fell matted and unkempt to their greasy shoulders. There were ladies in panniered skirts which were too wide for Boston's doorways and women in dresses which were hardly distinguishable from sacks. There were blood horses and draught oxen, aristocrats and beggars, patriots and poltroons, men in the service of the King and men wanted for desertion from the service of the King, in short, every variety and condition of man it is possible to imagine.

And there was, in Boston always, the Mob.

Mr. John Treegate, seated at his dining room table in his house on Edward Street, reflected upon these matters and

1

came to the conclusion that Boston was of all cities the true mirror of the world. He was Boston-born and proud of it; a solid figure of a man, broad in the shoulders, clad in sensible snuff brown worsted, conservative, sensible, prosperous and trusted.

He looked around at his guests, noted that their glasses were full, cleared his throat and rose.

"Gentlemen," he said, "a toast. I give you the glorious thirteenth of September, in the year 1759; the year and the day when we drove the French from this continent and made it forever British."

"The thirteenth of September," chorused his guests and drained their glasses. The men at the table had all been present on that day—members of the continental militia serving under General Wolfe. They had been laughed at by the Redcoats of the regular army, because of their ragged drill and lack of what might be called a uniform. But they had proved their worth in the face of the finest troops of France. And each year, on the anniversary of the battle, they met in John Treegate's house for a reunion dinner.

There were other toasts drunk—"Absent Friends," "The King—God Bless Him," "To Our Immortal Commander, General Wolfe," and "To Our Immortal Enemy, General Montcalm." And with these toasts came memories of that great day when John Treegate had first taken up his musket in defense of his king and his country to drive the French from the North American continent.

The French, at that time, lay around and above the city of Quebec on the Plains of Abraham, and the British Army, in transports, lay upon the river, repelled and daunted by the huge cliffs which they had first to scale before they could engage the enemy. The task seemed impossible, for every approach up those cliffs was guarded and it seemed that the British must withdraw without firing a shot and in withdrawing cede Canada to France.

And then had come the report that further up the river there was a goat track up the cliffs, nothing more than a tiny thread of pathway up which men could advance in single file, and General Wolfe had taken the decision to move his men up this goat track by night.

It was a tremendous gamble. Unless the whole army could move up this narrow lane, scrambling and groping in the dark, every man for himself, the British forces would be split in two. Half would be below on the river and half on the plains above facing the French and the result would be disaster.

But the gamble had paid off. By dawn John Treegate and thousands of his companions in the American colonial militia, and the British Redcoats and some regiments of Scottish Highlanders were atop the cliffs drawn up for battle, to the amazement of the French. There had been a heavy mist that morning, a mist which had helped in the scaling of the cliffs. When the sun had come up, this mist had turned into a shimmering white sea of silver, so that the men of Wolfe's command had seemed to be wading waist deep in surf. Then the sun rose higher and the mist went with the morning wind and half a mile away could be plainly seen the French in their blue coats—infantry, cavalry and cannon—a deadly harvest of them with the lily banner of France over their heads and bugles ringing with terrifying clarity to call them to arms.

At that moment, John Treegate had never been so glad for the presence of the British Redcoats. They had formed their lines as if all were but a drill and even when the French cannon opened fire, they showed no flurry or excitement but continued deliberately with their movements until they were ready for the battle, scorning either to flinch or seek cover.

"I doubt the world will see again such a charge as that of the Scottish Highlanders," said John to Eben Gawling who sat at his left. Gawling, who lived in the village of Concord, where he farmed a hundred acres, had come into Boston especially for this reunion dinner as he always did.

"They did well indeed," said Gawling, his voice booming out over the dining table so that all other conversation stopped. "They did well indeed. They were a noble sight to be sure, storming down upon the French stripped to the waist and their swords flashing over their heads.

"And yet I fancy," he continued, "that a nobler charge was that of the French, delivered against that sector of the British front confined to the care of the American militia. The Redcoats thought we would run and I'll confide to you, Treegate, that I thought we would run ourselves. They were an uncommonly unpleasant sight, the French—a solid line of them coming at us with the bayonet. Yet we turned them, sir. We turned them with musket fire and had we not turned them, I for one say that the day would have been lost."

"It was an opinion shared by many in the British command at that time," said Dr. Peter Wetmore, seated at the far end of the table. "I would be so bold as to say that without the service of the American colonials on the Plains of Abraham, this continent might well have been lost to Britain. We might all have been made subject to the King of France and forced to pay such taxes as would kill all commerce in these parts."

"And pray, sir," demanded a voice, "do you find matters so different today?"

There was a humming and hawing around the table, more of embarrassment than disagreement, and John Treegate turned to look at the speaker, who was seated beside his eleven-year-old son, Peter. Peter had been allowed to attend the reunion dinner for the first time, as a celebration of the fact that he had but that day signed his papers as an apprentice to the trade of barrel stave manufacture. And the man who sat beside him, and had asked the somewhat disagreeable question, was Tom Fielding, to whom Peter was apprenticed.

"I'm not sure, sir," said Mr. Treegate, "that I quite understand your meaning."

Tom Fielding cocked his head to one side, remarkably like a blackbird. He was a small man with long dark hair and reckoned somewhat too progressive for the merchants of Boston. He refused to wear a wig, for one thing, even on so formal an occasion as the present, and he kept up a lively correspondence with such men as John Wilkes, in England, who had been imprisoned for challenging the authority of the throne. Mr. Treegate was not entirely comfortable about having apprenticed his son to such a man, though undoubtedly the best barrel stave manufacturer in the city. But he was due to leave for England on the morrow and the apprenticeship was the only one he could manage.

"Why," said Mr. Fielding, "my meaning is perfectly clear if you will but face the facts. It is said that had we not beaten the French at Quebec, then we might all be paying heavy taxes to the King of France. And it is common knowledge that we pay heavy taxes—monstrously heavy taxes—to the King of England. Now, sir, what is the difference? Had we lost we would have been taxed and, having won, we are taxed nonetheless.

"Take my own business, sir. I make barrel staves. Barrels I may not make for it would interfere with the profits of the coopers of Bristol and London. So I must be content with making the staves. Now these staves, in the past, I shipped to the French West Indies and exchanged for molasses. And molasses I brought back to New England and sold here to be manufactured into rum. My profit came not from the sale of my barrel staves but from the sale of the molasses for which I exchanged them.

"And now look what has happened.

"I may no longer ship my staves to the French West Indies direct. They must first go to London and be put upon a British ship. Then they are sent to the French West Indies and have already cost me a pretty penny before I ever exchange them for molasses.

"And now comes the news that a tax of threepence a gallon is to be levied upon the rum made from the molasses. And all this done, mark you, by the King's ministers without anyone in these colonies being consulted.

"Well, sir. Is that tyranny or is it not? Would the French have treated us any worse?"

Mr. Treegate looked anxiously at his son, Peter. The boy seemed to be very much impressed by what Fielding had said, though he could hardly have been expected to have understood the half of it.

"These matters are too complicated for us to fully comprehend," said Mr. Treegate. "We have representatives in London discussing them and no doubt they will be listened to and what is just will be done. I go myself tomorrow to London on just such a mission. King George, God bless him, is no tyrannical French Louis."

"As to that," said Mr. Fielding, "all that has been done

so far is that more Redcoats have been sent here. And the temper of the people around the town is ugly.

"We have more soldiers in Boston than there are in London, I'll warrant, and we have to pay the expense of them."

"The people are in an ill mood with the soldiery," said Mr. Treegate, "because Sam Adams has made it his business to put them into such a mood. That man Adams is a ne'er-do-well and a danger to these colonies.

"He has failed in every business venture he has undertaken. He's a lawyer without a brief and a tax collector without either an office or a set of books. He wins people to his side by failing to collect their taxes. He spends his days in the city taverns consorting with the roughnecks of the streets and every idle apprentice. He is the king of the beggars and the rowdies and if he ever has his way we will not have order in these colonies but disorder.

"We will have not respect for authority but a horrible tyranny. We shall be ruled not by our betters but by our inferiors and all of us at this table will find ourselves taking orders from the drifters of Boston—the mob which is always with us as it is always in every big city of the world. With nothing to lose, this mob would have all others lose everything. We live, gentlemen, in the century of the mob, and it is against the mob that society must defend itself.

"Peter," he continued, turning to his son, "you may excuse yourself and get to your bed. You must be at Mr. Fielding's works at six in the morning, otherwise he will be more angry with you than he appears to be at the moment with the Redcoats."

Everybody turned now to Peter, their faces kindly and smiling. He got carefully down from the table and pushed his chair back in place.

"By your leave, gentlemen," he said as his father had taught him.

"Good night, young man," boomed Colonel Gawling, leading a chorus of good nights from the other guests.

Peter went quietly from the dining room. But he did not go directly to bed. He went instead to his father's study, brightly lit with half a dozen chandeliers. He tiptoed over to the fireplace and stared up at a gun in its bracket over the mantelpiece.

The gun was his father's musket; the same which he had carried at the famous battle of the Plains of Abraham. His father had put it on that bracket ten years before and announced that he would never use it again except to defend King and Country.

Peter loved the musket. It was the very essence of adventure for him. It had been used in battle and had witnessed the blue-coated French driving down on the continental militia, helping to drive them back. He got a footstool, climbed on it and reached up to the musket and touched the satiny polished stock. Beside the musket was a small picture of a man in a white wig. He wore the uniform of the continental militia and written at the bottom of the picture was *To my comrade in arms, John Treegate, with every good wish. George Washington. Colonel.*

Peter stayed several minutes in his father's study looking over the furnishings. It would be a long time before he saw them again for his father, during his absence in London, would close the house down.

When he tiptoed back past the dining room, he heard his father saying, "For rebels, sir, there is but one cure. The hangman's noose."

The boy had a hard time getting to sleep that night. His mind was occupied with his first day's apprenticeship with Mr. Fielding which was to start in the morning, and with the arguments he had heard at the dinner table, and with the discussion of Mr. Sam Adams, whom he thought must be one of the wickedest men in Boston.

And then he wondered about King George III whom he thought of in a red coat like the soldiers in Boston but three times as big as any of them. Plainly if a man were king he must be a giant. And he was busy with trying to picture his mother, who had died in his infancy, and getting her all mixed up with Mistress Polly who kept a sweetmeat shop on the corner, when he fell asleep.

Chapter 2

THE TERMS OF apprenticeship which existed in Boston, and indeed in all the American towns in those days, demanded that the apprentice be handed over completely to his master until he had served his time. Thus Peter Treegate, at the age of eleven, left his father's home on Edward Street, the large, comfortable, well-furnished house, with a fireplace in every room (a notable feature, this), and went to stay with his master, Thomas Fielding.

Physically the exchange was a poor one. In his father's home, Peter had had a comfortable room in the top of the house, with a bed of which the mattress was as fat as a cloud with goosefeathers, and a fine chest of drawers in which to keep his clothing.

At Tom Fielding's place, however, he shared a room with two other apprentices and had a truckle bed with a very thin mattress. The room, at the top of the house, was badly in need of repairs and chinks in the wooden walls allowed the wind to come through so that the room, hot and stifling in summer, was in winter piercingly cold.

Peter found no fine chest of drawers in which to keep his

clothes and other belongings. All he had was a small box at the foot of his bed and this was not provided with a lock.

The two other boys were Ephraim Blake and Joe Golding. Ephriam was sixteen and in the final year of his apprenticeship. He had learned all the tricks of his trade and a few others besides—among them the appearance of doing a good deal of work and being prodigiously busy while actually doing nothing. He seemed at all times to have quite a quantity of money and, being a senior apprentice, was not obliged to be in his bed at eight o'clock each night. Frequently he did not get to his room until the clocks of Boston were striking midnight and, when he returned as late as this, surprisingly he came through the window.

This happened the very first night Peter slept at Mr. Fielding's.

He was awakened by a scuffling on the roof and saw, in the pale square of light made by the curtainless window, a grotesque figure fumbling with the latch. Peter, sure that robbers were entering the house, was about to shout when Joe Golding rolled over in bed, cocked a sleepy eye at the window and whispered to Peter, "It's Blake coming back. Pretend to be asleep or you'll be sorry for it."

But Peter was so surprised that he was still half sitting in bed when Blake, having got the window opened at last, came into the room. Blake was beside Peter's bed in a second and seized the boy by the front of his nightshirt.

"What did you see?" he hissed, shaking Peter vigorously.

"You coming in through the window," Peter spluttered.

"Oh, no you didn't, you little worm," said Blake. He slapped Peter across the face with the back of his hand and then immediately clapped the palm over the boy's mouth lest he cry and awaken Mr. Fielding.

"Now," he hissed, "what did you see?"

Peter could not reply because of the hand over his mouth and Blake shook him again.

"What did you see?" he demanded.

"Nothing," said Peter, the word bumbling through the other boy's palm.

"That's better," said Blake. His mood changed immediately. He sat down on Peter's bed and said almost gently, "You're new, ain't you? Well, the most important thing you've got to learn is never peach on another apprentice. No matter what he did, never peach on him. Understand?

"Now don't blubber. There's no women here to dry your eyes. Here. Take this." He reached in his pocket and took out a piece of stale currant cake. Peter didn't want the cake, but he took it and thanked Blake.

"You got a mother?" Blake asked suddenly.

"No," said Peter, "she's in Heaven." This was what his father had always told him about his mother, and he made the reply quite naturally.

"Well," said Blake, "that's a consolation. Your father in Heaven too?"

"No. He lives on Edward Street. But he's on his way to England and my brother, Stephen, who is five, is going to live with my aunt in Philadelphia." Peter volunteered all this information in the hope that it might promote the friendly attitude of Blake. But the effect was quite the contrary.

"I don't want to hear all your confounded business," he snarled. "I don't want to hear about your father and your little snot-nosed brother. Just remember you ain't seen nothing." He reached out in the gloom and gave Peter's nose a sharp twist as if his nose was the key to his memory and by twisting it he had locked the door.

Blake now turned to the other boy, Golding. "You asleep, Goldie?" he asked.

Goldie made no reply.

"I know you ain't asleep," said Blake. "But I don't know whether to thump you or leave you be. I think I'll leave you be tonight. Your turn next time."

And with that Blake sat heavily on his own bed, removed his boots and, without undressing further, went to sleep.

As for Peter, he spent most of the rest of the night in sleepless fright and loneliness—loneliness so intense that it brought a pain in his throat and his chest. He cried a great deal, doing his best to make no noise in fear of waking the unpredictable Blake. But Blake snored on. Eventually Goldie comforted him.

"Hey," he whispered. "I'm cold. You can come over in my bed if you want. Bring your blankets." Peter didn't know whether Goldie did this because he was really cold or out of friendliness. He got into the other boy's bed and Goldie said, "You got to learn not to cry if you're going to be a Boston 'prentice. You got nothing to cry about, really. It just looks bad now the first night. And Blake will be leaving in seven more months."

"I hate him," said Peter.

"Not half as much as he hates himself," said Goldie.

Mr. Fielding's apprentices, of whom there were but the three already named, followed a rigorous and undeviating routine each day, to which Peter was introduced on the following morning.

He was awakened by Goldie throwing him out of bed and saying, "Wash, get dressed and make your bed. Ten minutes until prayers."

There was a basin in the corner of the room containing some water and, beside it, a bar of soap, very strong (being more lye than fat), and an extremely dirty towel.

Peter staggered drowsily in his nightshirt over to the basin and meanwhile Goldie busied himself with putting the boots on the feet of the still sleeping Blake. Peter had not quite finished washing himself before Goldie pulled him away from the basin to take his own turn at it, at the same time shouting to Blake that but four minutes remained before prayers.

Blake groped his way off his bed, pushed Peter and Goldie aside, went to the washbasin, slapped a little water on his face and bawled immediately for the towel. The room might have been big enough for one boy to dress himself in with some comfort. It was much too small for three, and Peter found that he could get his clothes on only by standing upon his bed, balancing precariously as he struggled into his knee breeches.

Somehow the three were ready on time and even had a minute to straighten their beds before going to the second floor of the house, where prayers were conducted for Mr. Fielding, his family and his apprentices by the Reverend Eustace Perks.

These prayers took but ten minutes and consisted largely of an impassioned appeal to Almighty God by the Reverend Perks that all apprentices should continue in hard work and duty to their masters and beware of the corruption of money, the corruption of the world's goods, the wiles of female companionship and the pit of taverns and brawling.

During this exhortation, Peter stole a glance at Blake, who had upon his face a look of piety which would have done credit to an angel. His was the loudest "Amen" in the little congregation and he was the last to leave the little chapel, as if loath to turn his back upon spiritual comforts and face those corruptions of the world against which he had been so recently warned.

Peter thought that he might have breakfast now, for he was feeling extremely hungry. But first came schooling—two hours of it which lasted from six until eight and during which education contended with hunger for attention, and the hunger of the eleven-year-old boy readily gained the upper hand.

Mr. Fielding conducted the class on unique lines. He elected to teach history, geography, reading, writing, ciphering and poetry and prefaced his lessons by announcing that the curse of commerce and, indeed, of civilization was the ignorant apprentice and the ignorant tradesman.

"The foundation of all government is education," he said. "Without education both of rulers and the ruled, government becomes tyranny. Mr. Blake, you will kindly recite for me the kings of England starting with the Angevin dynasty."

Blake, who had a quick memory, rattled his way through the Plantagenets and Angevins, the Houses of York and Lancaster, the Tudors and the Stuarts and the Hanoverians as if he were reciting the multiplication tables.

"What do we learn from these many changes in the ruling House of England?" Mr. Fielding demanded of Peter.

Peter blushed. He had never given the matter a thought and was stumped for an answer.

"We kept running out of kings," he replied lamely.

Blake gave a snort of contempt. Mr. Fielding turned on him coldly.

"The answer is quite correct as far as it goes," he said.

"It would be fully correct if Master Treegate had said that England kept running out of *suitable* kings. Mark the word 'suitable.' It carries a world of significance. For from the time of the Stuarts it has been the people of England who have in the main decided who shall rule them.

"An unpopular king might once have retained his throne as a result of the ignorance of the people and the brutality and power of the king's retainers. In the reign of King George III, that is no longer possible. An educated and vigorous people will no longer put up with tyranny either in England or in these colonies here."

These latter words were said in a thundering shout, as if Mr. Fielding was intent upon making his views known not only to his little class but indeed to the whole of Boston and London. Peter felt uneasy at the words. They smacked of what his father would have called treason.

From history, which had somehow become politics, Mr. Fielding switched to ciphering. But this also became politics when the fiery master described how the measure of one foot had been based on the size of the foot of one of the early English kings.

"Greater nonsense it would be hard to imagine," he stormed, "than that the whole of linear measurement should depend upon the size of a sovereign's boot." With geography it was the same. Geography started with the source of the River Thames. The course of the river was traced until it reached Westminster, when the river was abandoned for a discourse on the corruption of the English Parliament. And so with every subject. Whatever the starting point, the finishing point was the same—politics and the need for the sharpest vigilance against tyranny.

"They call him Tyranny Fielding," Goldie whispered to

Peter when they left the classroom.

Finally, to Peter's enormous relief, breakfast was served. This was eaten with the Fielding family and presided over by Mrs. Fielding. Peter had never met her before, and indeed she proved a very difficult person to meet. To be sure he *saw* her and was introduced to her: a tall thin woman, all angles, so that her sharp nose was matched by the sharp elbows of her thin arms, and the sharp line of her long jaw.

But though she might physically be present in the room, it soon became clear to Peter that mentally she was in another world. She went vaguely about the business of putting the food upon the table, and all the time her head was cocked to one side as if she were trying to hear something which was being said in a whisper by someone above her, presumably someone embedded in the ceiling.

This attitude of straining to hear on the part of Mrs. Fielding was so marked that Peter glanced once or twice at the ceiling to see whether there might not be something there which he had missed.

During the meal, Mrs. Fielding said once or twice to the room in general, "They are very quiet this morning," and this produced no effect at all upon Mr. Fielding who would reply quietly, "Are they, my dear?" and go on with the business of the meal.

Toward the end of this meal, conducted in silence except for the odd remarks of Mrs. Fielding that things were very quiet that morning, the good lady turned to Peter and seemed to notice him for the first time, though the two had already been introduced.

"Who is that boy?" she demanded of her husband, pointing her bony finger at Peter.

"The new apprentice, my dear," said Mr. Fielding. "Master

Peter Treegate."

"He is a disturbing influence," said Mrs. Fielding. "That is why they are so quiet this morning. Boy, do you believe in spirits?"

"Say 'yes,' " whispered Goldie.

"Yes," said Peter.

"It's quite all right," said Mrs. Fielding, addressing the ceiling. "He believes in you. Unbelievers are a most disturbing influence. The spirits will not be in the same room with them. You may kiss me, boy."

Peter, blushing, got up from the table and went around to Mrs. Fielding, kissing her with great caution on her thin cheek. "There," said Mrs. Fielding to the ceiling. "He's a friend, you see. You may return now and speak to me of the great unknown."

"My wife is a spiritualist," said Mr. Fielding.

The woman, deserting the ceiling for the moment now that the spirit world had been mollified, turned her vague grey eyes on Peter.

"How old are you?" she said.

"Eleven, ma'am."

"You are very small for eleven." She clapped her hands and out of the kitchen came a slovenly girl of whom Peter had, up to that moment, caught only glimpses.

"See that this boy has potato soup with his dinner every night, Agatha," said Mrs. Fielding. "He is not the right size at all." She turned once more to Peter.

"Potato soup will not interfere with your spirituality," she said, "though you may find it a little binding on the bowels. I have many children," she continued. "Spirit children. They are better than physical children. They don't die."

And then she gave a quick sob and walked out of the room.

Chapter 3

THE BARREL stave factory of Mr. Fielding comprised a large and unheated building to which no architectural planning had ever been devoted. The building had originally been three structures—a stable, a coach house and a blacksmith's shop. The stable had been of wood, the coach house of wood and local field stones, and the blacksmith's forge was wholly of stone but stone so sooted over that the walls appeared to be of the same iron which the blacksmith had worked.

These three structures, each with its own floor and its own roof being adjacent one to the other, Mr. Fielding had converted into a factory for the manufacture of barrel staves. Outside was a large yard, covered in a haphazard manner with tarred felt, sacks, sheets of iron and any material which would come to hand. In this yard, known as "the forest," planks of ash, pine and oak, from which the staves were cut, were put in racks to season.

There were whole cliffs of these planks, rising ten or fifteen feet in the air with air spaces between them every three feet. Peter soon found that "the forest" was a fine place in which to play.

The planks were worked in the factory in a primitive assembly line. They came in at the stable end where they were cut into required lengths under the supervision of the cutting foreman. They went from there to the coach house area for rough shaping and to the old blacksmith area for final shaping and bundling.

Mr. Treaser, a small grey man in his sixties, so thin that he seemed weighted down by his ragged clothes, was in charge of the apprentices. He had once been a cabinetmaker. He lost no opportunity to point this out and made it clear that he was engaged in his present work only as a stopgap measure, because of the heavy unemployment in Boston.

Nonetheless, the stopgap work had lasted fourteen years and seemed likely to last to the end of Mr. Treaser's days. Mr. Treaser, as became a cabinetmaker, wore an apron of green baize about his waist and upon his head a hat made of paper, in the shape of a box.

Whenever he required to write anything down, Mr. Treaser took his hat off and made the necessary entry on it, so that his paper hat was a mass of figures and memoranda such as "twelve score oak hogshead staves by Friday." Mr. Treaser made himself a new hat each Monday and transferred to it any unfinished business from the old. Peter came to the conclusion that if Mr. Treaser were to lose his hat upon a Wednesday, the business of Thomas Fielding, Cooper, would come to a standstill on the following Thursday morning.

Peter was handed over to Mr. Treaser for his initial training in the trade of cooper. The little foreman, so grey of complexion and hair that he seemed perpetually covered with a light hoar frost, operated on the assumption that all boys knew nothing. He regarded himself as the only complete repository of knowledge in the art of woodworking. And he was in no hurry to share this knowledge with his apprentices. He doled it out in the tiniest amounts, as the captain of a ship, short of supplies, might scrupulously ration water to his crew.

For the first few months of his apprenticeship, Peter did nothing but sweep out the shop, run errands, fetch saws, planes, drawing knives and other tools, clean them at the end of the day's work, and help in bringing in the required planks from "the forest" at the start of each day. At the end of this time, Mr. Treaser took Peter aside for an examination.

"Bring me," he said, "a shaving of red fir."

Peter did so and was then sent for a shaving of Carolina pine, English oak, and western spruce—"western" being the remote part of the colonies beyond Philadelphia. When he had brought and identified these shavings, Mr. Treaser pronounced himself grudgingly satisfied.

However, he had more tests to come. He gave Peter a piece of red fir and said, "Point out to me the wet years experienced by the region in which this tree grew."

This demand for what seemed impossible knowledge stumped Peter, to the great satisfaction of Mr. Treaser. He delivered a lecture on boys who wasted their apprenticeship learning next to nothing, said that if the future of woodworking depended upon boys like Peter, the outlook was hopeless and then undertook to supply the answer himself.

"When it rains a great deal," he said, "a tree grows fast. It adds one ring to its growth each year. When the distance between the rings is great, it was a wet year. When the distance is small, the year was dry. You are not qualified to buy lumber unless you know this."

"Thank you, sir," said Peter.

"If you don't know, ask," said Mr. Treaser. And then he snapped, "But don't come bothering me with silly questions." That concluded the examination and Mr. Treaser took off his paper cap and put a note on it, this being, Peter assumed, the results of his test on his first six months as a cooper apprentice.

Peter had undergone a far harder test in the first week of his apprenticeship. This consisted of his admission to the Benevolent and Rebellious Fraternity of the Apprentices of Boston. Blake inaugurated these proceedings as the senior apprentice in the Fielding manufactory.

"Be out on the south side of the Common at six this evening," Blake said. "If you fail, it will be the worse for you."

Peter asked Goldie what this meant and Goldie went white. "They're going to admit you to the Boston apprentices," he said. "Get some cloths and put them in the seat of your breeches. Don't worry. I'll be there."

Peter was sick with anxiety all day, but got to the Common at six as Blake had told him. There was a crowd of thirty or forty boys there—all apprentices and all ragged and tough-looking. There was a hogshead on the ground and Blake was sitting upon this with a barrel stave in his hand.

"There you are, shaver," he cried, spotting Peter. "Bring him here, brothers, in the approved manner."

The apprentices immediately seized Peter's legs and frog-marched him on his hands to the foot of the barrel.

"First for baptism," cried Blake, plainly delighted with the prospect of some fun. He jumped down from the barrel and took off the top. It was full of foul water, and Peter was picked up and plunged struggling into this and held under so long and by so many hands that he was almost drowned before he was allowed to bring his head above water.

"Cold?" demanded Blake.

Peter, frightened and sobbing, blubbered that he was.

"We must warm our brother up," said Blake. "Make a back, somebody." Several boys offered their services, going on their hands and knees. Peter was thrown over the back of one of the kneeling boys and Blake picked up his barrel stave and belabored him unmercifully on the buttocks.

Peter, almost hysterical with fright, trembling both from this and the cold, was not greatly hurt by the beating, thanks to the cloths he had put in his breeches. But the faces of the dancing boys around, who were grinning and jeering at him, and shouting, "Hear how he howls," were more terrible than the barrel stave.

They were all older boys, of about the same age as Blake, and seeing the terror on Peter's face, this moved them not to pity but to delight in his suffering.

Someone shouted, "Raise him now. Raise him now," and the shout was taken up by others. The beating ceased and Peter was thrust onto a large square of sailcloth. The apprentices grabbed the edges of this and started tossing him up in the air, higher and higher until he was sure that he would miss the sailcloth sometime on coming down. What happened, however, was worse than that. Blake yelled, "High enough," and the boys let go the sailcloth. Peter, at that point, was perhaps seven feet in the air and was allowed to tumble to the ground, his fall unbroken. He hit the grass all arms and legs, the wind knocked completely from him, and lay quiet.

"He's out," someone said.

"We must revive him," said Blake.

Some water was dashed over him and Blake dragged

the boy to his feet. "You're wet," he said. "And cold. That's a shame. You must run around the Common until your clothes dry."

But at that moment there came a shout from beyond the crowd of apprentices and someone cried, "Here's the Suckling Babes."

What the Suckling Babes were Peter soon found out, for into the mob of bigger apprentices charged a horde of smaller boys, few older than twelve or thirteen, but all armed with cudgels, barrel staves and axe handles.

They were led by Goldie and a free-for-all broke out, with rocks and sticks filling the air, and boys tumbling and punching at each other on the ground. The melee lasted for perhaps ten minutes and Peter's only contribution, frightened as he was, was to try to get out of the way. In this, however, he was not successful, being confronted, as soon as he got up, by one of the bigger apprentices who knocked him to the ground.

He struck out ineffectually, as one fights in a nightmare, each blow curiously lacking any force, but finally there was a shout of "Watch! Watch!" and the combatants fled, Goldie stopping only long enough to drag Peter to his feet and help him away.

They went to a ramshackle hut on the eastern side of the Common, in a neighborhood of dilapidated buildings. This hut was apparently the rallying point of the Suckling Babes, for soon a dozen or more of them had collected there, most of them bruised and cut, breathing hard, but their eyes bright with excitement.

"Sorry I couldn't get there any sooner," said Goldie. "I had a hard time getting enough of us together."

He looked around at the others who had collected. "This

is Peter Treegate," he said. "Mr. Fielding's apprentice. He's new and one of us."

The others examined him in silence, those in the rear standing on tiptoe to see him over the shoulders of those in front. Peter was still blubbering, his shoulders shaking in massive sobs because of the shame and the terror to which he had been exposed. The sight of him awakened in each of the boys memories of their own condition when they had been subjected to the ordeal of initiation as a Boston apprentice. They were painful memories and each secretly tried to assure himself that he had not sobbed so much as the boys before them. But the effort was not successful.

"Quit crying," said one of them roughly. "You ain't dead."

"I caught Blake a good crack," said another. "With a stone. He'll have a cut over his eye." This latter had himself a welt on his face which, in the light of the hut (someone had produced and lit a penny dip), was already showing blue.

"You got a knife?" demanded a third of Peter.

Peter could not find the voice to reply so shook his head.

"Here," said the boy. "You can have this 'un. I got two. It's a good knife."

He pushed a worn Sheffield clasp knife into Peter's hand. The knife had at one time been faced on the handle with sheep bone, but on one side the bone had come off. Through his tears, Peter examined it and the unexpected gift and the generosity behind it steadied him. "Thanks," he said.

"You got to remember that you're not alone," said Goldie. "It's when you think you're alone that it's really bad. But you've got us. We're the first- and second-year apprentices. We're called the Suckling Babes. That's Blake's name for us. The older apprentices follow him. He calls them the Pot Wallopers.

"We just watch out for each other. If any of the Pot Wallopers gang up on you just shout 'Babes' and some of us will come and help. Understand?"

Peter nodded.

"Good," said Goldie. "Get out of them clothes and we'll dry them. Then we'd better get back to Mr. Fielding's. We'll be late for supper."

Peter, shivering, took off his clothes and the drying consisted of two of the boys wringing them out as hard as they might. This did not make them much better than damp and they were uncomfortable and awkward to put on again. But Peter now felt a glow of warmth arising out of the comradeship of the other younger apprentices and was ashamed that he had cried so much.

For Goldie his feeling was one of hero worship, the feeling a small boy has for a big brother, though Goldie was but a year older than Peter.

Dinner was already on the table when they returned and Blake in his place with a cut over his eye, the edge of the cut turning blue. Mr. Fielding eyed his two young apprentices and noted the rumpled wet clothes on Peter. He looked at Blake and scowled.

"There are times when I feel sorry for you, Mr. Blake," he said. Blake was astonished and a dark shadow of fright came into his eyes, for he was afraid of his master.

"Why?" he asked.

"Because you are a bully, sir," said Mr. Fielding. "And a bully is one who seeks to convince himself that he has courage which he hasn't got by abusing those weaker than himself. Yours must be a very unhappy state of mind," he concluded. "I would not like to live in your condition."

If Blake was prepared to make any reply, Mr. Fielding gave him no opportunity. "Agatha," he called and the worn and ragged Agatha popped her untidy head out of the kitchen, a huge saucepan in her hand wreathing her in clouds of steam. "Take this boy's clothes off in front of the stove," said Mr. Fielding, "give him a good rubbing down, fill him full of hot soup and get him to bed." He turned to Peter. "Did you cry much?" he snapped fiercely.

"No," said Goldie quickly. "Not much, really."

Mr. Fielding turned to Goldie and, though he tried to appear stern, he could not disguise the affection he had for the boy. "Master Golding," he said, "you cannot indefinitely undertake to champion the whole world. This boy and other boys have to do most of their growing up themselves."

In all this exchange, Mrs. Fielding had remained pecking at her food, her head cocked to one side in her curious listening position. She was in another world and when Peter had been dried and fed and sent to bed he reflected that he had that day been in another world—one of whose existence he had not dreamed when he was in his father's house.

And he wondered how many other worlds there were in the familiar city of Boston.

Chapter 4

THERE WERE IN Boston a score of other worlds of which the boy, Peter Treegate, caught an occasional glimpse in his walks around the city on errands for Mr. Treaser, the foreman, or in his work at the cooper's premises of Mr. Fielding.

There was the world of the lieutenant governor, Thomas Hutchinson, who lived in the stately Province House not far from the Old South Church. An uneasy world this, full of anxieties for the lieutenant governor. Whatever he did that was agreeable to Boston was disagreeable to the Ministry in London.

Peter saw the lieutenant governor several times; once when His Excellency was on his way to church. He sat in the back of his coach upright and pale, dressed in sober black and with a cascade of lace at his throat. As the coach clattered along the street, only a few people raised their hats. Stones were thrown at it and jibes shouted. And the lieutenant governor sat in his seat, staring straight ahead at the back of the coachman, like a man who expected no more pleasure in the world.

Another time, the lieutenant governor's coach was blocked behind a drayman's cart and immediately a crowd collected around. There was always a crowd in the Boston streets, for unemployment was high. At first the crowd contented itself with staring at the governor. And then one or two people climbed on the back of the coach, jostling off the footmen.

In a few minutes they had taken complete possession of the vehicle, and someone had scrawled on the side the words WORK NOT TAXES.

Peter, caught in the mob, was lifted by a friendly laborer upon his shoulders to get a better view of the fun and saw the man who did the writing. He was a bold-eyed, blocky-jawed man and the mob around moved aside to let him do his work.

"That's Sam Adams," said the laborer. "Hurrah for Sam," and the hurrahs followed with enthusiasm.

Peter had, before his father's departure for England, heard him talk of Sam Adams. He was the man his father identified as the leader of the mob and a rebel; someone who, in his father's view, should be hanged.

"Let me down," cried Peter, for he was afraid of even being a spectator at such proceedings.

The laborer lifted Peter down, but it was only to put him at the feet of the very man, Sam Adams, of whom he stood in such terror. Squirming to get out of the mob, he jostled Adams' legs and the man turned around and caught sight of him, lifting him up, kicking and protesting.

"Put me down," shouted Peter. "Put me down." But Mr. Adams either did not hear him or elected to take no notice. At that moment, Lieutenant Governor Hutchinson decided he had better get out of his coach and did so with some difficulty. He confronted Sam Adams and in a moment silence descended on the crowd.

"Mr. Adams," said the governor, "I would be glad of your assistance in getting through this crowd. I have business to attend to at the State House."

"I have no control over the people," said Adams.

"I have heard differently," replied Hutchinson.

"You are the King's representative," said Adams. "Ask them to disperse in the King's name."

The lieutenant governor glanced around at the grinning faces of the crowd. He returned to Adams and to Peter's horror eyed him closely. Adams had him on his shoulder.

"Your son?" inquired the governor.

"A Son of Liberty," said Adams.

"I'm not a Rebel," piped Peter, afraid that the governor might have made a note of him as such. "I didn't want Mr. Adams to pick me up. I'm a loyal subject."

"It seems, Mr. Adams," said the governor, reaching up for Peter, "that you take more upon your shoulders than you have the right to."

"My father fought for the King at Quebec," said Peter, anxious not to be taken for a traitor. The mention of the battle gave the governor an idea. He mounted the step of his coach, facing the crowd, and called out, "Will all those who bore arms in duty to their King in Canada render now a further service to their sovereign by permitting me to go upon my way."

"Long live the King," somebody shouted, and the cheers which followed were as loud as those which had been given but a few minutes ago for Mr. Adams. The drayman's cart was got out of the way, the governor returned to his coach, the footmen returned, much rumpled, to their stand on the back, the coachman whipped up his horses, and the vehicle rattled at high speed down the street.

Peter went home puzzled. The crowd had cheered for Sam Adams and defied the governor. The crowd had cheered as heartily for the King and defied Sam Adams.

What was it all about?

He couldn't decide and knew of no one to ask who would give him an explanation. He approached Mr. Fielding but was rewarded only with a harangue on tyranny, taxation, the Townshend Acts, the Stamp Act and a host of other matters which had little significance for him.

A second world of which Peter Treegate, Boston apprentice, caught a glimpse and wondered at was the world of the soldiers, the British infantry, referred to always as the "lobster backs" or the "bloody backs."

Two regiments of infantry were stationed in Boston—the 14th West Yorkshire and the 29th Worcestershires. Peter knew the difference between the two. The West Yorkshires had pale buff facings on their lapels and the Worcestershires a deep yellow. Nobody seemed to have a good word to say for the soldiers. They were universally despised and hated.

A month after Peter had started his apprenticeship, a man came to the factory. He was a tall man and thin, with a face which seemed to have been much out in the weather, but which had never become accustomed to this exposure. It was red and raw and the man was dressed in ill-fitting clothes which were equally ill-assorted. His breeches were a dirty grey and his coat had once been a purple velvet, the coat of a gentleman passed on through many hands until it had reached its present scarecrow owner. The lapel of one of the big French pockets had been cut off to provide a patch for the garment. Where there had once perhaps been big silver buttons, with the coat of arms of a nobleman embossed on them, there were now but pieces of string tied through the buttonholes.

This scarecrow, for all his wretched outfit, had nonetheless about him an air of neatness, and he approached Peter who was at the time in "the forest," clicked his heels, made as if to salute, and then recovered himself and ended with a half-hearted touch of his forelock.

"Axing your pardon, young sir," he said, "but would there be any work around here to do?"

"I don't know," said Peter. "You'll have to ask Mr. Fielding in the office."

At that moment Blake appeared. "A lobster back," he shouted. "I can spot 'em a mile away. Out with you, you rogue, trying to take the work away from honest men of Boston."

"I'm just looking for odd jobs, sir," said the man, who had winced at the words "lobster back."

"Nothing for you here," said Blake. "Out before I throw you out."

"What's all the confounded noise," said Mr. Fielding, appearing.

"This bloody back here," Blake said, "has come whining around looking for work. I've told him there is no work in Boston for the likes of him."

"That's right," snapped Mr. Fielding.

"Thank you, sir," said the soldier, touching his forelock again. And he added, "No offense meant." He turned to walk out of the lumberyard but, before he reached the gate, Mr. Fielding stopped him.

"How long since you earned tobacco money?" he asked.

"Two months, sir," said the soldier.

Mr. Fielding pointed to a pile of wood shavings and sawdust, bark, leaves, mud and stones which had collected in one side of the yard.

"If you are prepared to move that out and dump it in the river," he said, "you may have a shilling."

"Thank you, sir," said the soldier. He took off his coat to reveal an extremely ragged shirt of flannel. Peter thought he would certainly keep this on, for the day was chilly. But apparently the soldier's pathetic suit of civilian clothes, in which he could look for work, was very valuable to him, for he took off the shirt as well. Bare to the waist, he then set to upon the pile with a fork and barrow.

He worked hard and without taking any rest, loading the barrow and trundling it off down the street, keeping very much to himself, so that Peter could hardly get a word out of him. He wanted to know why a king's soldier had to do menial work for tobacco money and he wanted to make it clear to the soldier that he, Peter, did not bear him any hard feelings.

When the soldier had finished his work, which he did in a remarkably short space of time considering the size of the pile he had to move, he cleaned the barrow and the fork, put on his tattered shirt and his caricature of a coat and presented himself to Mr. Fielding for his pay.

The latter gave him his shilling and the soldier asked whether he might come back again, perhaps in a month's time, when there would be the same job to do.

"No," said Mr. Fielding. "It's against my policy to employ you lobster backs. I made an exception in your case."

The soldier sighed. "I understand," he said. "But dooty's dooty."

Peter was careful to be present at this interview, still curious about the soldier.

"If you cared to leave your present service," said Mr. Fielding casually, "I fancy the colonies are big enough to—er—hide you."

"That would be desertion," said the soldier.

"It would," said Mr. Fielding.

"A hundred lashes if caught—if you're lucky," said the soldier. "Otherwise six feet of rope and six feet of air." He made a circle around his neck and jerked his thumb upward in a graphic pantomime of a hanging.

"You should not submit to such tyranny," said Mr. Fielding. "Come. How did you come to join the King's service?"

The soldier grinned, revealing a mouthful of yellow teeth. "Through drinking beer at Leed's fair," he said. "A sergeant give me a tankard of beer to drink the King's health and when I'd drained it, why, there was a shilling in the bottom. And that meant I'd taken the King's shilling and so I become a soldier.

"Fifteen years ago, that were." He turned and looked at Peter.

"That being the way in which you were dragooned into the army," said Mr. Fielding, "you should have no compunction at leaving at the first opportunity."

"There's them hundred lashes," said the soldier.

"You have heard, I suppose, of the saying 'Better to die free than live a slave'," said Mr. Fielding.

"At times I gets fits of deafness," said the soldier. "I got one of them right now and ain't hardly heard nothing that you're saying to me. That being so, I can't repeat nothing that you said to anybody. Thank you for the work, sir." And with that he went out.

Mr. Fielding shook his head. "Poor fellow," he said, "he has forbidden himself the right to think. Make sure that fate never overtakes you, boy."

Peter was about to go but Mr. Fielding detained him. "I have had a letter from your father," he said. "He has arrived safely in England but tells me that his business is likely to detain him not four months as he had expected but a year." Peter's disappointment showed immediately in his face and Mr. Fielding sought to comfort him.

"The time will go quickly enough," he said. "I am writing your father to say that you show promise in your work and are a credit to him. Is there any particular message you would like to send him?"

Peter shook his head. How could he tell his father, through another, how lonely he felt, and about the apprenticeship initiation by Blake and how profoundly his life had changed.

"Nothing," said Peter, not because he had nothing to say but because he had too much to say.

"Very well," said Mr. Fielding. "Back to your work."

The winter of 1769-1770 was a hard one. Snow fell in Boston as early as October. It remained on the ground through November, December, January and February.

It was shoveled by householders and businessmen from the fronts of their houses and premises into the middle of the street, and pushed from the middle of the street to the front of the buildings by the traffic of coaches and carriers. There was a suggestion made that the Redcoats garrisoned in the city be employed in the removal of the snow. But nothing came of this. The snow was everywhere and interfered with everything—the social life of the women and the most pressing duties of the men and the city officials.

In March this same snow became a political weapon, a surprising weapon indeed.

From the time of the first heavy snowfall that winter, it became the practice of the Suckling Babes, under Goldie, to snowball any members of the Pot Wallopers, under Blake, whom they could find. Often mass snow fights between the two groups took place on the Common during which bricks and chunks of ice were thrown as well as snowballs. The more respectable people of Boston avoided the Common, for they were likely to get snowballed themselves if they ventured near the apprentices. But Sam Adams who, Peter found, seemed to take an interest in every activity of the city, however minute, often stood on the outskirts of the battle watching these fights.

He seemed to take an especial interest in them, cheering neither side but watching intently. And, after one especially active fight, he invited Blake, Goldie and Peter to his house for a dish of tea. Peter didn't want to go, distrusting Mr. Adams, but went anyway, because of Goldie.

"You young rascals have good sport on the Common," he said. "But I could suggest better sport for you."

"What's that?" asked Blake.

"Well, now," said Mr. Adams, "how about a few snowballs for some of the bloody backs on sentry duty around the town? I fancy there would be something to laugh at in seeing them dance and dodge and unable to do anything about it."

The apprentices had often snowballed the Redcoats before. Indeed, anybody they saw was a fair target and that included Lieutenant Governor Hutchinson.

"That would be nothing new for us," said Blake.

"I suppose not," said Mr. Adams. "Well, it was just a suggestion."

Peter was never sure whether this little conversation had anything to do with what followed a few days later in King Street.

He was passing along the street one evening, returning from an errand for Mr. Fielding, when a boy fled past him yelling, "Run, run." Peter believed that the Pot Wallopers must be on the boy's heels and set off down the street with him. The boy darted up an alley, leaving Peter running on ahead, whereupon someone seized him by the scruff of the neck and dragged him to a halt.

He was whirled around and found himself facing a soldier. "Snowball the captain, would you?" said the Redcoat. "Little brat. I'll teach you some respect for authority. Take that." He backhanded Peter across the face, knocking him to the ground, and then, when Peter tried to rise, knocked him down again with the butt of his musket.

Two or three people quickly gathered and someone shouted, "Let the boy alone." The soldier glared at them, hesitated, and with another scowl at Peter marched back to his post. The boy was quickly hauled to his feet.

"Why did he hit you?" someone demanded.

"I don't know," said Peter. "I didn't do anything."

"Pushing our lads around now," said another.

"Blasted bullies," said a third.

"We'll show 'em," said another. "Come on. Let's go to the barracks on Water Street." None of these people who had so suddenly collected were decently dressed. They were what Peter's father called ne'er-do-wells and loafers—in short, the Mob. They wanted Peter to come with them, but he refused and went off to Mr. Fielding's.

But that night, after dinner, as the boys were in their room, they heard a great deal of running and shouting in the street below. Shivering in their nightshirts, they looked out of the window down to the street and saw, flowing over the snow like a black river, a crowd of people, some walking, some running, some proceeding by little hops and jumps of excitement in the direction of King Street. Blake, as usual, was out and Goldie said suddenly, "Come on. Let's see what all the excitement's about."

They dressed quickly and got to the street by Blake's route, which was well known to Goldie. This consisted of walking over the flat roof to the far side and jumping a gap of two feet to the roof which covered Mr. Fielding's lumber yard.

From this, they lowered themselves over the side to a stack of planks a few feet below and so got to the ground. It was easy to open the lumberyard gate and get into the street—a street alive with excitement. It was packed with people all going toward King Street and calling cheerfully to each other by name, promising good sport before the night was out.

Some of this excitement gripped Peter and Goldie and, fearful of arriving too late, they ran through the crowd to find that in King Street, before the Customs House, there was a huge mob already collected.

The mob, apprentices and loafers, were baiting the lone sentry who stood outside the Customs House. Snowballs were being flung at him and chunks of ice too, and the soldier dodged and jumped as best he could, bereft of all military bearing.

With the missiles came taunts and insults. "Picking on boys, eh?" someone shouted. "Daren't face men, though." Suddenly Peter realized that he was the cause of all this disturbance, and felt at the same time fearful and enormously flattered.

"Go on back to England," said another. "We don't want soldiers here."

"Bullies!" shrieked a woman in a shattering falsetto. "Tyrants! Thieves!"

"Let's tar and feather him," said another.

"Throw him in the river."

"No, drag him around through the snow. That'll cool his military ardor."

All this while the snowballs and the chunks of ice flew thick. The unfortunate sentry ducked and dodged and brought up his musket in a pretense of firing, a pretense which had no effect upon the mob except to incite them to further efforts.

At last the sentry had had enough of it. "Guard!" he bellowed. "Guard! Guard ho! Help!"

Then there came the sound of drums and the crisp command "Right wheel" and around the corner from Brattle Street came a squad of Redcoats led by a captain.

For a moment the mob recoiled, easing nervously across King Street to the other side, opposite the Customs House. The Redcoats formed a single file facing the mob. The crowd was near enough to see the faces of the soldiers and they were not impassive faces.

Their eyes were angry and they had a look about them of men bent on vengeance. Every one had, without a doubt, been subjected to numerous insults by the Boston mob. They had, while on sentry duty, been pelted with bricks and snowballs and ice chunks and they had a score to settle.

Several, without orders, raised their muskets to the firing position. Their captain, John Preston, knocked the muskets down with his cane.

"There will be no firing unless I so order," he shouted.

"You daren't fire," someone shouted from the crowd. That shout broke the spell. The mob had retreated across the street, afraid and unsure up to that moment. Now Peter saw a snowball pelt through the air and hit one of the soldiers on the face. It was followed by a score more and to these were added a few cobblestones.

"Get back," roared Captain Preston. "Get back. I order you to disperse in the King's name."

But the crowd was in no mood to listen. It had been frightened and had now found its courage again and, ashamed of his previous fear, each man was determined now to show himself as bold as his neighbor.

The mob surged forward and those in the forefront found themselves only a few feet from the muzzles of the soldiers' muskets. Peter and Goldie were thrust forward in this manner.

The roar of the mob increased and the soldiers brought their muskets up again, glancing at their captain. But he struck them down as fast as he could, passing along the line of his men and shouting to the crowd to disperse. Then one of the soldiers, struck on the chest by a clod of ice, lost his footing on the slippery ground and fell.

Peter wasn't quite sure exactly what took place then. There was a roar and a flash of musketry—a bright yellow stab of light which lighted up the faces of the soldiers and those in the forefront of the mob for an instant. Several men in the crowd slumped to the ground and patches of blood appeared on their ragged shirts and stockings. The blood looked black in the moonlight. Peter had, to get out of the line of the muskets, wriggled to one side with Goldie. He looked from the soldiers to the mob, the whole scene now illuminated by a deathly white moon in the dark hard sky of winter.

Captain Preston had thrown himself upon his men and was pushing them back, shouting to them not to fire and belaboring them with his cane. There were more drum rolls and a further squad of soldiers rounded the corner and poured into King Street. The mob recoiled, leaving four or five of their number inert on the snow. One man, with a shattered leg, whimpered pitifully and dragged himself toward the crowd. Two darted out from it and lifted him to carry him to safety.

Then on the balcony of the Old State House, which lay at the end of King Street, only about four houses away, Lieutenant Governor Hutchinson appeared. He shouted for silence and, in the shock which followed the discharge of the muskets, he was able to make himself heard.

The mob, Peter knew already from the scene involving the governor's coach, had no love for the man. Yet he calmed them with a few words, promising a full and impartial investigation of the night's affair.

"Leave the matter in my hands," he shouted. "Go to your homes lest there be more bloodshed. I pledge my word that justice shall be done and done immediately."

And so the crowd melted away, taking the dead and the wounded with them. The soldiers returned to their barracks. And standing alone in the street, when Peter left, was Sam Adams in his worn coat and patched stockings.

There was a patch of bloodied snow at his feet and he looked from this up to the balcony of the Old State House where Lieutenant Governor Hutchinson had stood.

He didn't say anything, but Peter knew that some day

there would be a terrible reckoning between the forces the two men represented—the Mob and the Law. Or could it be the People and Tyranny? Peter did not know.

Chapter 5

ALL BOSTON was buzzing like a beehive overturned the next day, with the news of the killing of five men and the wounding of six others by Captain Preston's soldiers outside the Old State House. Of the six wounded, two died in a very short while and the death roll thus standing at seven, the common name given to the event was "massacre."

It seemed like a massacre to Peter. He was very much frightened by it. He had never seen a man dead before, let alone a man killed by musket shot with the blood flowing from him like claret from a bottle. And all this because some snowballs had been thrown at a sentry. It was a terrible vengeance when thought of calmly. Peter was haunted by the belief that he himself was the cause of it all and he begged Goldie not to mention to anyone that they had both been present during the massacre.

As far as he knew, nobody at Mr. Fielding's knew anything about the incident between himself and the soldier before the massacre took place. He had not told Goldie of it nor anyone else. He determined to keep the matter to himself for to be the cause of seven deaths was a dreadful thing, and he was sure that if it were found out, he would most certainly be hanged.

He remembered something Mrs. Fielding had said to him a few weeks before. "Boy," she had said, "you are covered with blood." The statement, coming without warning, had startled him. He wondered whether he had unknowingly cut his hand in working with the cooper's tools. But he found no blood on himself and concluded that Mrs. Fielding was repeating something which had come from the spirits. Now it seemed that he was covered in blood indeed. And it was the blood of other people.

The terrible thought that he was responsible for the killings weighed most heavily upon him, and the more details of the massacre he heard, the more wretched he felt.

He could not help hearing details. The story was the main topic of conversation in the city for days. Men who did not even know each other joined other men who did not know each other at the corner of any street to discuss the slayings.

Sometimes fist fights broke out in the streets over the issue. The ragged Boston mob was all against the soldiers, and it was only some of the richer sort who supported the King's men. And yet some of these, notably John Hancock, the wealthiest merchant in Boston, denounced the slayings in plainest terms and said they gave not a fig for any government which enforced its decrees with musket shot.

The day after the killing, the news was all over Boston that the eight soldiers with Captain Preston had been arrested and were to be charged with murder.

"And if there is any justice in the world," said Mr. Fielding, "they will all of them be hung for bloody-minded rascals. And good riddance to them."

Sam Adams brought this news to Mr. Fielding. He was an occasional visitor at the Fielding house, never stopping for long, and usually only to spread some item of news he had gleaned in his constant journeyings around the city.

"The troops are all to be withdrawn to Castle William in the harbor," said Mr. Adams. "I had it out with Governor Hutchinson myself. 'Leave more of your soldiers around this city,' I told him, 'and there will be more of these slayings. They are hated by the populace and rightly, and they themselves hate the people. You will bring about a bloodbath, sir, if you leave another Redcoat in the streets of Boston. I will not be answerable for the temper of the people.'"

"And what did he say to that?" asked Mr. Fielding.

"Why, he said he'd think about the matter, and I told him there was a time for thinking and a time for action and now was the time for action. He had the troops moved within the hour and sent for me to say that Preston and his men are to stand trial."

Peter had climbed atop a pile of lumber in the "forest" adjoining the window of the room which Mr. Fielding used for his office and he could hear every word that was said plainly.

"How did all this start, Sam?" asked Mr. Fielding.

"There's a hundred versions," said Mr. Adams. "But the essence of the matter seems to be that one of the Worcestershires chased a young lad, cuffed him to the ground and then clubbed him with his rifle butt. Several saw this happening. I've questioned them closely. The story got about and the mob became incensed against the Redcoats. They had every right to be incensed, sir. Our women have been reviled, our men shouldered off the streets and our premises and businesses searched and searched again by this set of scoundrels saddled upon us in the name of law and order.

"Law and order indeed! They rehearse their bands outside our Boston churches during divine service and make a mockery even of our worship. They took up their quarters in the most cherished buildings in this city, eat our food, abuse our people and now they take to bullying boys. There will be no peace in these colonies while there is one British soldier on duty here."

"About this boy," said Mr. Fielding. "It seems to me that if he could be found and a statement taken from him, matters would look very black indeed for these eight soldiers. Mind you, I am not a man to stand by and see injustice done, Sam Adams. I don't want men hung who are guiltless of any fault but the strictest observance of their duty. But I am with you in that I do not like to conduct my business under the barrel of a musket, so to speak."

"If we could find the boy," said Adams, "I believe there would be nothing left for the court but to find the soldiers guilty of unprovoked abuse and unprovoked bloodshed of the civil population. And find the boy we will, sir. I have men out looking for him at this moment. He is vital to our presentation of the case."

Peter now found himself in a terrible situation. He fully believed that he had been the cause of the massacre, and it now seemed that his testimony might lead to the hanging of the soldiers. He was covered in blood indeed, as Mrs. Fielding had said.

He did not know what to do nor whom to turn to for advice.

Mr. Adams had said the soldiers would certainly be hung

as the result of his testimony. Peter was too young to know of the fiery exaggerations characteristic of Sam Adams. All he knew was that his father had said these soldiers were, many of them, the same who had fought beside him at the Plains of Abraham.

Whom to turn to then? Peter had no friends in Boston other than Goldie. And Goldie was down at the wharf making inquiries about the arrival of a barge with a shipment of timber.

Mr. Treaser, the foreman, was useless, Peter knew, as a source of advice. He was probably the only man in Boston who was completely unmoved by the killings. He lived in his world of wood quite remote from the affairs of men, his only concern being that no bad barrel staves were produced by the Fielding factory while he was foreman.

Peter had a miserable day of it, several times deciding to go directly to Mr. Fielding and make a clean breast of matters, and as many times checking the impulse and resolving to be quiet.

Goldie returned shortly before dinner, but Peter had no chance to speak to him. Immediately after dinner, Mr. Fielding announced that he was going to a meeting at Sam Adams' house and he would require someone to light his way with a lantern and be available to run any necessary message.

"You may come if you wish, Peter," said Mr. Fielding, and Peter's heart sank. He was quite sure that there would be someone at the meeting who would recognize him as the boy who had been beaten by the soldier.

Sam Adams was a shabby man and lived in a shabby house. Of all the strange citizens of Boston, he was certainly one of the strangest. He came of a good Boston family and, like his cousin John Adams, had been educated at Harvard.

But where John had turned his education to good account, becoming the greatest lawyer of his day in Boston, Cousin Sam had done little with his education. He had no buttons to his coat which he kept fastened with pieces of string. His stock, even when it was clean, was never ironed. His woolen stockings drooped down his legs. He was missing the buckles on his shoes which like his coat were fastened with pieces of string.

Yet this ragged man was a friend of the richest merchant in Boston—the proud, handsome and influential John Hancock. More than that. Though his official position was that of a petty collector of taxes, he was one of the few men in Boston who could see the lieutenant governor any hour of the day he pleased.

Among the tradesmen of the city as well as among the unemployed, he was the most popular man in Boston. He knew the names of hundreds of Bostonians, some of them men whose homes were warehouses and sail lofts and shacks of moldering board and canvas. Each of these got a "good day" from Sam Adams when he met them in the streets.

All men mattered to this shabby man.

Peter recalled a story he had heard of a man who lived in Paris many centuries before, and who had organized the beggars of the city and saved it from attack. He had been called the "King of the Beggars." And Peter decided that Sam Adams was the king of the beggars also, and from then on always thought of him as such.

The room in Mr. Adams' house in which the meeting was held was small and so poorly furnished that chairs had to be borrowed from next door to seat all the gentlemen attending.

There were a dozen or more of them, far too many for the tiny room, and Peter was crowded into a corner where he found a small stool and sat on it, his feet tucked underneath so as to be as much out of the way as possible. From this position, he got only the strangest view of the gentlemen who were seated around the table—the back of the neat white wig of Dr. Joseph Warren, part of the red cheek and equally red nose of bluff James Otis, a glimpse, beyond the candles, of the open frank face, crowned with long dark hair, of a man called Revere, and beside him the shoulder only (for his head was hidden in shadows) of a big man called Sullivan, who had come to Boston all the way from New Hampshire.

Sam Adams opened the proceedings and, after thanking the gentlemen for meeting with him at such short notice, gave them the news of his visit to Governor Hutchinson, the decision to move all the soldiers to Castle William in the harbor, and the further decision that the eight men and their captain must stand trial for murder.

These tidings were hardly news to the men in the room, but they were receiving them officially from Adams who, for all his untidiness, was certainly the leader of the group.

"And now, gentlemen," he said, "we must consider the significance of this event and what is to be done in respect to the future. The significance is plain. The soldiery can no longer be tolerated in Boston or anywhere in these colonies. They must be got rid of—completely. All must, as I see it, unite in a demand that they be removed to England."

"Why are you so harsh against these Redcoats, Sam?" asked Dr. Warren. "Do not recite to me the list of the various hardships they have imposed on the city, culminating in this frightful butchery. I know them all. What is your deeper reason?"

"A simple and basic one, sir," said Sam Adams. "The soldiers are here to enforce compliance by the people of Boston to laws which the people of Boston have had no hand in making. We are, sir, to put it plainly, ruled by the musket. We have no vote in the passing of laws. If we protest against them, it will be at the peril of being shot. And that, sir, is Tyranny. No other name will serve."

He spoke quietly but with an intensity of feeling which left a deep impression on the gentlemen around the table, and even Peter found himself stirred.

"Is it not possible that they are here only temporarily in any case," said Dr. Warren, "and that they will be withdrawn when matters are more settled?"

"Withdrawn!" cried Adams. "And for how long, sir? Until some other incident such as the Stamp Act, or the abominable taxations of that blackguard Townshend, are reimposed upon these colonies by the parliament in Westminster? And then what will happen?

"We will protest, will we not, as we have a right to protest as free men. And what will follow?

"Why, more ships of war in Boston harbor, more Redcoats landed on the Long Wharf and quartered in Faneuil Hall and the Old State House. And more massacres in the streets of Boston.

"What the rulers in London are doing is not only depriving us of representation, of the right to vote. They are also depriving us of the right to protest.

"A more unnatural state of affairs the world has never before seen, sir."

There was a grunt from the end of the table where the big man Sullivan was seated. Peter leaned forward on his stool and caught a glimpse of the Irishman's head appearing out of the shadows into the candlelight. He sat so tall at the table that the candles lit only the underparts of his face so that his forehead was in shadow, but his cheeks, chin and nose were brightly lit and the effect was almost frightening.

"I will beg leave to differ with you, Mr. Adams," said Mr. Sullivan. "For in the country of my father, Ireland, which I call the fourteenth Atlantic colony, matters are in a worse pass than here. There a man may not own a horse over the value of five pounds, he may not own a weapon with which to defend himself, nor buy or sell property for profit, nor school his children as he will, nor meet in groups of more than five.

"And all this enforced at the point of the musket, for the nation is teeming with Redcoats. You see the Irish arrive here daily as refugees from their own country. They are a testimony of what tyranny is, when fully enforced."

"But that is a matter of the control of the rebellious and obnoxious Papists," said Mr. Otis.

"Papists be blown!" roared Sullivan, pounding the table with a huge fist and his face glowing red like a coal in a fire. "The freedom of a man is not something to be given or withheld on the basis of his worship. You are not to have one law for the Papists and one law for the Protestants. Men are men, sir—Irish, English or Hottentot. Papist, Episcopalian or Plymouth Brother. God alone may judge of the state of men's lives and their immortal souls. Repress one group and you have at a later time an excuse for repressing another. Liberty is not divisible, sir. It is the common heritage and birth right of all men."

"I had not intended to offend," said Mr. Otis.

"I take no offense," said Sullivan. "But if it is right to

garrison Londonderry, then it is equally right to garrison Boston. What protest we make here must be not for Boston alone, but for every city in every colony under the control of Britain. And I will make so bold as to add every city and every people who find themselves oppressed in any part of the world."

"Ah," said Sam Adams. "Now we get nearer to the nub of the matter. For it is not the liberties of the people of Boston alone that are at stake here. It is the liberty of the people of New York and of Philadelphia and of Charleston, and of every city and town and settlement in these colonies. And these people in these cities and places must be made to see that.

"They must not come to think, as they may readily be made to think by their various governors and king's agents, that it is only because we in Boston are rebellious and stiff-necked that we are garrisoned with troops. All must be made to see that our cause is theirs and their cause ours—that the soldiers in Boston deny *them* the right of protest as they deny us."

Dr. Warren smiled gently and nodded his neatly wigged head. "I suppose you have a plan as always, Sam?" he said.

"I do," said Adams. "It is a simple one. We must see to it that news of everything that takes place in Boston is fully and accurately known all over the colonies. We must see to it that anything that occurs elsewhere is fully and accurately known here."

Sullivan snorted. "You will do nothing with newspapers," he said. "They are too readily suppressed or bought with the King's gold."

"I don't propose a newspaper," said Adams. "I propose

what we might term a Committee of Correspondence. Several gentlemen in this city will undertake to write letters giving the story of our troubles, which will be printed and circulated throughout the colonies. Gentlemen in other cities—New York, Philadelphia and so on—will do likewise. Thus there will be a free and ready flow of information throughout these colonies. And the governors will not be able either to suppress the writing of these letters, nor bribe the authors to cease writing them."

"And what about the acts of sedition and libel?" asked Mr. Warren.

"A skillful letter writer may slip through these without trouble," said Adams. "You do not have to use your own name in any case. A pen name will suit admirably."

"And who will see to the distribution of these letters?" Otis asked.

"I will," replied Adams. "Give them to me and, with the aid of Mr. Revere, I will get them around. And I will write to my friends in Philadelphia, New York and elsewhere and ask them to join in the plan. We have already, Mr. Revere and I, made a start on this plan for spreading our news to all the people of these colonies. Do you have your sketch with you, Mr. Revere?"

Up to this point, the silversmith had not taken any part in the discussion. He now reached inside his frock coat and took out a roll of paper which he smoothed open on the table, to reveal a colored sketch of the troops firing into the Boston crowd. The men around the table stood up to look at it and grunted their approval.

"Mr. Revere is to engrave this upon a copper plate, and send as many copies as he can around the colonies," said Adams.

"It is a spirited rendering of the scene," said Otis.

"I have never seen a better piece of work," said Sullivan.

Revere gave an elaborate shrug and then smiled at them in the candlelight.

"I do not deceive myself that this is art, gentlemen," he said, "but I will hazard that this drawing will have a bigger effect upon the world than many a painting by a far more eminent man."

The meeting had convened at Mr. Adams' house at seven that evening and it was still going strong at nine o'clock when Mr. Fielding glanced at his watch. The room was stuffy and hot and Peter, worn out by the excitements of the day, had dozed off on the little stool in the corner.

Mr. Fielding leaned over to him and shook him by the shoulder. "Peter," he said. "Peter. I am likely to be held later than I thought. You had better get back home to bed. Take the lantern with you. One of these gentlemen here will light me on my way."

Peter took the lantern, put on his cloak, bid good night to the company and went out into the street. The sky was clouded over and there was a howling wind whining and moaning through the town. It made the signs outside the shops creak and groan on their hinges. Across the street, a shutter slammed with a report like a musket. Peter jumped with fright. A dog howled and a man came reeling out of a tavern roaring that he must be on his way. He had a lantern with him but, being considerably under the influence of spirits, dropped it and it went out in the snow.

"Plague take it," said the man and kicked the lantern. He spotted Peter. "Ho, boy," he shouted. "Here. Light me home and I'll give you a shilling."

The man staggered toward Peter and grabbed him by the shoulder. "Now, boy," he said. "Take me to Number 36, Long Wharf. You shall have a shilling for your pains, as I said."

He pushed Peter forward, still holding tightly to his shoulder, and indeed he had need of the support, being unsteady on his feet. Peter had no choice but to guide the man who attempted to make a rhyme out of the fact that he was going to pay a shilling for light, but the task proved too much for him. Instead he contented himself with shouting snatches of song and taking ineffectual swings with his stick at the moving signs of tradesmen's shops as they passed beneath them.

The wind, if anything, blew the harder during the journey, whipping up clouds of powdery snow. People had shuttered their windows against the fierceness of the weather, so that there was no light in the street but that made by the lantern.

When they got down to the docks, which lay in the rough end of the town, the man stopped and looked around him, peering through the blackness and the flying snow.

"Do you see anybody, boy?" he shouted above the wind to Peter.

"No," Peter replied.

"Four hundred yards more," said the man, "and you shall have your shilling. Come." And he pushed the boy forward again.

Chapter 6

THE LONG WHARF, as its name implies, was one of the principal jetties or piers of the city of Boston, thrusting out into the river. Along one side of it were a number of houses, huddled together as if holding hands and in desperate fear of tumbling off into the water. The lower parts of these houses served by day for storage sheds for cargoes landed from ships and also as accounting offices for ship's clerks and others engaged in tallying such cargoes. Their upper floors were in many cases residences. Many merchants lived above their own counting houses on the Long Wharf and Peter assumed that the man he was guiding was a merchant.

The place, busy enough in the daytime when the wharf itself was often blocked by carts and hand barrows and other traffic, was always deserted at night. There was a lone light at the far end of the wharf as a guide for rivermen, but otherwise the place was unlit. And being unlit and but poorly patrolled by an incompetent watch, it was a favorite hangout for roughs, thieves and drunkards, rivermen, sailors and stevedores, many of whom were prepared to break a head or two in the hope of gaining a shilling.

It was for this reason, Peter knew, that the man he was guiding had peered about before setting foot upon the Long Wharf and asked whether they were being followed. Once on the wharf, there being no side streets, there was no way of escape if the two of them were set upon by rowdies. And many a man returning alone from a night of carousing in the taverns of Boston had had his head broken and his purse cut on the Long Wharf.

The two then set out upon the wharf where the wind, no longer impeded by buildings, swept viciously over the water, bringing a driving snow with it straight into their faces. It was a wicked wind, this, full of startling tricks.

It caught hold of a small barrel, rolled it suddenly out of the dark ahead, straight at the two, who stood for a second paralyzed with fright to see such an object come hurtling out of the gloom at them. The barrel touched Peter's legs, veered by some quirk of the wind, and went crashing into one of the buildings to the side.

This same wind next seized a large tarpaulin, which it lifted up into the air and sent sailing and flapping like a huge bat across the wharf to disappear in the darkness over the water. It caught at gutterings and raised a devilish tattoo, banging them against the eaves, and flung tiles from the houses and hammered on shutters.

All the while the wind howled and groaned and moaned so that Peter, on the exposed wharf, had to hold his lantern under his cloak to prevent its going out.

This brought its light into his eyes, partially blinding him, and he now got some comfort out of the hand of the man still gripping him by the shoulder.

But then, when they had struggled but a hundred yards

along the pier, Peter felt another hand on his other shoulder; he was whirled around and in the next second thrown to the ground, his lantern going out.

He heard the man with him roar "rascals" and caught a blurred picture of him staggering back and falling and of three men belaboring him with cudgels. The man tried to rise and had got to his hands and knees, his coattails flying over his head in the gale, when one of the attackers struck him in the back three times and with a cry of "I'm done for," the man settled, face down, in the snow.

Peter was too frightened to move. He wanted to get up and run. But he knew that if he did he would be quickly overtaken by the ruffians and perhaps thrown into the river.

So he lay still and the three men, one of whom had a lantern, turned their victim over and quickly went through his clothes. They evidently found a great deal of money, for they were soon stuffing their pockets. Then, not content with these spoils, they proceeded to drag the clothes off their victim, flinging him around as if he were a sack. They had reduced him to his underwear before one of them shouted:

"What about the boy?"

"He's run," said another.

"No, he ain't," said the first, holding up his lantern. "There he is."

The third of the three, who had not spoken, grabbed the lantern and came over to Peter. He lowered the light over the boy and their two faces were illuminated in the little yellow glow which it gave out. Peter gasped.

"Blake!" he said. So that was the reason that Blake was always out so late at night and had so much money to spend.

He spent his nights robbing drunken men returning to their homes from taverns.

"Why, you little spying rat," said Blake and grabbed Peter and shook him fiercely with one hand, as if by shaking him he could make him disappear so that he would not be a witness to what had taken place.

The other two came over. "You know 'em?" one said to Blake.

"Yes, curse him, I know him. And he knows me, perish his soul. The little spying sneak thief." And he started shaking Peter again.

"What are you going to do?" one shouted above the roaring of the wind.

"Do?" cried Blake. "Why, knife him and throw him in the river. The dirty little spy." And again came a shaking, even more vigorous than the first two, so that Peter's head was swimming and he was breathless and could not say a word.

"Where's my knife?" asked Blake suddenly.

"It's over there in the snow," said the other. "I'll fetch it." He took the lantern and returned in a minute with a big clasp knife. Peter recognized it immediately. It was the same knife the boy had given him after his initiation into the Boston apprentices. He had missed it a few days later from his chest, for there was no lock on the chest.

"That's my knife," he exclaimed, his senses returning a little. It was an odd thing to say in view of his peril, but the knife had been Peter's most precious possession, and he had missed it sorely.

Blake looked at the knife and then at the man huddled in the snow. His figure could barely be seen on the edge of the light of the lantern. Already the snow had started to drift around the body and Peter knew that the man was dead.

"Why, so it is," said Blake and his face changed from anger and terror to cunning. "So it is. It's your knife. And everybody knows it's your knife. And you know what that knife done? It killed a man. Your knife. Killed a man. That's murder." He threw the knife suddenly at Peter.

"Come on," he said suddenly to the others. "Leave him here with the stiff. I'm in the clear. 'Tis the boy's knife. And we three can swear we never set foot on the wharf this night."

In a moment they had gone, leaving Peter in the snow with the bloody knife and the dead man. The boy did not know what to do, for he was so terrified he was incapable of thinking.

His first instinct was to run to Mr. Fielding's house for help and he got to his feet with that intention when it occurred to him that Blake would be there.

Or, more likely, Blake might be waiting for him somewhere along the way and would kill him.

He looked down toward the landward end of the wharf. He could see nothing but it seemed to him that in the howling blackness down there would be Blake and the other two men and they would pitch him in the river if he tried to get by.

He looked at the shuttered and dark houses around. Perhaps he should hammer on one of them until he aroused someone, and tell them what had happened.

He tried at one door but could make no noise which was not completely drowned by the wind and the rattling of shutters and the general fury of the storm. He was alone then with a man who had been murdered. The world seemed to have withdrawn from him, to be looking at him aghast as the

world did look at murderers. Once again, as Mrs. Fielding
had said, he was covered with blood. He tried to dispel his
rising panic by thinking of his friends—Mr. Fielding and
Goldie and even the foreman Treaser. He was prepared, in
his anxiety, to count even Sam Adams as a friend, though
he looked upon him normally as a rabble rouser.

But all these people with their help and support and
comfort were divided from him by the black streets of gale-
stricken Boston. And the boy was convinced that somewhere
in one of those streets, or in an alleyway or doorway, or more
likely right at the foot of the pier, Blake would be waiting
for him with murder in his heart.

And this man, about whose body the snow danced and
whirled, had been killed with Peter's knife; a knife which
many people knew belonged to him.

One impulse now gained the upper hand and that was to
get away from the pier and the dead man and the horrible
knife which Blake had thrown upon the snow where it was
soon buried.

He dared not go by land, and that left only the water.
He searched along the side of the wharf, peering into the
black depths below where the river splashed and gurgled,
and finally came to a slippery ladder leading down to the
water.

From where he stood, Peter could not see the bottom of
the ladder, but he decided that there just might be a boat
moored there, for plainly the ladder was used by boatmen.

Down he went and found a small and clumsy boat tied to
a piling near the ladder. He was in it in a trice and worked
with hands trembling with anxiety to untie the frozen ropes
which tethered the boat to the pier. There were two of these
ropes, for the boat was moored fore and aft to prevent its

being smashed against the pilings.

It was a terribly hard job to undo the moorings, for often the boat, swung by wind, tide and river, pulled the ropes taut so that they were as rigid as bars of iron. But at last he had the boat free, and it was immediately caught by the tide and the downflow of the river and banged against the pilings. It tipped on one side, nearly throwing the boy into the water, got free, swirling around, bumped upon another piling, got caught broadside to the flow of the water and nearly filled, got free again, and so went on its way under the wharf until it got clear on the other side.

Peter had never been in a boat before, but he had some idea of rowing from having watched watermen in the river. But the river now was rough and choppy and he could not see even the length of the boat. Whirled around end for end in the dark, with the waves frequently breaking over the side, and the terrible wind driving snow like a whiplash into his face, he soon had no idea where Boston lay, whether to the right or the left, or straight ahead or behind him.

For fifteen or twenty minutes he struggled with the oars, but it was purposeless work, for he could give no direction to the boat which he sensed was being carried out to sea. Then, quite suddenly, a shape loomed out of the dark toward him, and grew monstrously bigger with the passing of each second. He heard, even above the noise of the storm, a brisk splashing and hissing and the voice of a man, far away and tattered as a rag, crying, "Clew up them topsails."

And then, a cliff, or so it seemed, swept down the river and struck Peter's little boat, driving it before it through the water, until the water piled up and the boat sank.

Peter leaped desperately as the boat went down under him, and grabbed in the blackness overhead for whatever there might be to hold to. His hands caught a freezing chain, slippery with ice and, with the water sucking at his feet, he nearly lost his grasp.

But black fear gave him strength, and he held on, the bow wave of the ship—for such it was—rising at times over his waist and even to his shoulders. It was this that saved him, for he was floated up by this wave and so got a better grasp upon the chain, hooking his arms over it.

But at this point his strength failed.

He lay there almost dead from cold with the water rushing over him and after a little while it seemed to him that it was not cold any longer but warm. He began to feel drowsy and almost comfortable except for the chain which cut him under his arms and across his chest.

Then there was a faint glow of light over his head and someone said, "There's a boy on the bobstay." Two strong hands reached down and he was lifted up into the air and swung over upside down and thrown, full length, upon the deck of the boat.

He looked up into the glare of a lantern and saw above it two men in oilskins peering down at him.

"Ain't dead," roared one.

"Close to it though," said the other. This latter reached down and jerked Peter to his feet, holding him upright by his long hair with one hand, and thrusting the lantern in his face with the other.

"Douse that glim," roared a voice from out of the darkness and the lantern was immediately extinguished. "Take him below," the voice ordered and Peter was dragged across the deck and then down a companionway into a hold.

There was a post in the center of this hold (the boy found out later that it was one foot of the mast) and on it, hanging by hooks, an enormous quantity of coats and breeches, hats and mufflers. Around were a number of bunks and one of the men motioned to these.

"Get them clothes off," he said, "and dry yerself. Here." He reached to the post and took from it a grey piece of sackcloth. "Use this," he said.

With that, the two of them withdrew. Peter, trembling both with cold and a deep fear from what he had witnessed on the pier and also the belief that the murder would certainly be blamed upon him, was incapable for a while of doing anything. He just sat on one of the bunks, fighting down panicky thoughts which surged upward in his mind, like demons arising from a pit, to haunt him.

They ranged all the way from the Boston massacre to the fact that he was now upon a ship, patently bound out of Boston, and was, in short, running away from his master and thus violating the terms of his apprenticeship, though against his will.

Eventually all the terrors and pitfalls which surrounded him, all of them the product of the last twenty-four hours, proved too much for the boy. He flung himself on one of the bunks and cried out of sheer desperation and friendlessness. He was still crying, shaken by huge sobs which were uncontrollable, when one of the men returned.

" 'ere," he said. "What's this. Can't have crying aboard a ship. 'Tain't no place for it at all, at all."

He dragged Peter off the bunk and forced the boy to face him, but the big sobs were by no means to be controlled and shook his whole frame.

"Lord," said the man. "I'd ha' thought you was wet enough without adding to it with tears. Does yer chew tobaccy?"

Peter made no answer to this astonishing question and the

man took a roll of canvas out of his sou'wester, unwrapped it and exposed a black quid of tobacco. Off of this he cut a morsel with his knife, as if the tobacco was the most precious substance in the world, and gave it to Peter.

"Have a chaw," he said. " 'Twill do you good."

Peter got control of himself, put the tobacco in his mouth and bit on it. Immediately a large quantity of saliva formed in his mouth, hot and acidic, and some of it slipped down his throat. He coughed and spluttered and spat out the tobacco. His limbs felt for a moment as if they had been seized in a vise and his head spun. A sweat broke out on his face and he sat down weakly on the bunk, convinced that he was going to die and not in the least sorry about it, so long as dying did not take too long.

"Reckon you don't chaw," said the seaman. "Well, 'tis a nasty habit, the Lord knows. But when there's a shout for 'All hands' look you, and it's a matter of taking in the royals in a hard blow, and so dark ye couldn't see the devil if he was sitting on the yard beside you, and you eighty feet up in the air, why then, I wouldn't be without my quid. No. Not I. Nor most seamen. 'Ow old are ye, boy?"

"Eleven," said Peter.

"Why, you're next door to being a man. I was a mate—a mate, mark you, when I was fourteen. And I'd a been a captain now but for one thing."

"What's that?" asked Peter.

"Cain't neither write nor reckon. Learned the alphabet once though as far as *m*. Then come that other letter that's a first cousin to an *m*. What's its name again?"

"*N*?" asked Peter.

"Ah. That one. That one always threw me. They didn't ought to have two letters that sounded so much alike. Makes a hard job of learning, that does, *m* and *n*. No seaman would have done it that way. Seamen is practical people and they'd have called one of them *m*, see, and another of them some other name mighty different."

"Like what?" asked Peter, for the man had a steadying, rustic kind of voice and spoke so calmly and slowly that some of Peter's terrors left him for a while.

"Well, like Jack or George, maybe. *L, M,* Jack . . . that'd be a sight easier to rememberize and help a whole lot of people out of their ignorance. You says you're eleven. What's your name?"

"Peter Treegate."

"You know," said the man, "I wouldn't say you was much of a young feller for running off at the mouth. Here I bin talking to you for nigh on ten minutes asking you questions and listening real patient and keeping me mouth shut and me ears open like me father told me (him that had a good farm at Ilfracombe; that's in Devonshire in England) and all I got out of you is that you're eleven and your name's Peter Treegate. That ain't a Devon name. Nor it ain't a Cornish name either. You must be from maybe Somerset or Hampshire."

"I'm from Boston," said Peter.

"Ah well," said the man, "they got all kinds of names in Boston. But ain't you going to give with a little more information—like what you was doing in that boat?"

The mere mention of the boat brought all of Peter's terrors back in a flood into his mind and the man, seeing the boy's eyes go bright with fear, headed him off.

"No need ter talk if you don't want to," he said. "But the captain will want to know. He sent me here ter find out something about you. 'Gabby,' he said—me name's Gabby,

Gabby Jukes, though where I got it from I don't know for I'm a silent man meself. 'Gabby Jukes,' he said, 'step into the forecastle there and find out something about that boy. And don't take the whole watch about it,' he adds. So you see, I gotta know something about you.

"Why don't you just tell me, and I'll hold back anything you don't want the captain to know. You can rely on me, me being a silent man."

While Gabby was by no means a silent man, he seemed a kindly one, and Peter had too much locked up inside to keep to himself much longer.

He told Gabby the whole story, starting with the soldier chasing him, so that he believed he had set off the massacre in Boston, and ending with the murder and how he had taken the boat to get off the wharf and land somewhere in the city where he could avoid Blake.

Gabby heard him out to the finish and then shook his head. "You're in trouble," he said. "Too much trouble for a boy. You need a father, that's what you need. And you say your father's over in England, though you don't say why. Still, no doubt he's got his reasons, for a man would hardly go to England without there being a good one. But seeing as you said and I said that your father's in England and you need a father, why then, I'd better throw you a line and take you in tow.

"And the first thing I got to say to you, in my stint as acting father is this—Don't you say nothing about this here murder to nobody. Not nobody. See? You was picked up in the boat because you got into the fool thing for a lark and off it took you down the river. You understand that, now, boy?"

"Yes, sir," said Peter.

"Had a boy of me own," said Gabby. "He was a pagan

boy because his mother were Chinese, but he were just as nice as any Christian boy I ever see."

"What happened to him?" asked Peter.

"Ain't nothing happened to him," snorted Gabby. "He grew up, that's all. Come on. Get them wet clothes off you."

Chapter 7

PETER SLEPT heavily the whole night through, a sleep of utter exhaustion, and when he awoke all his terrors returned to him, and added to them the new terror of being on a ship bound he knew not where. He was not given much time, however, to reflect upon his troubles, for shortly after dawn Gabby tumbled him out of his bunk and, unwashed as he was and in rumpled, ill-fitting clothing, took him to the captain.

The captain was not in his cabin but up on the quarter-deck cowering in the lee of a strange little half shelter that stood to one side of the deck. The whites of his eyes were red and on his cheeks there was a glistening of salt from the sea spray which had dried there in the wind. His whole figure was clothed in a shapeless oilskin cloak which reached to his leather seaboots. And this oilskin, a dirty olive shade, had deposits of salt in the innumerable wrinkles which covered it.

But the strangest feature of the captain, whose name was Pleashed, was that he wore upon his head a turban instead of a cocked hat. And this turban had itself been waterproofed (by coating it with linseed oil and hanging it to dry in the sun, Peter found later) so that it looked as though Captain Pleashed had a beehive upon his head for a hat.

The wind was still blowing briskly but there was no snow, and Peter's conversation with the captain was held in a shouted exchange to carry above the wind, which at sea made sounds far different from those it made on land.

"Do you know aught of the sea, boy?" roared the captain above the wind.

Peter shook his head.

"Why, blind your eyes," roared the captain, "what do you mean coming aboard my ship and knowing naught of the sea?"

"He's powerful anxious to learn, he is," roared Gabby. "Never seed a likelier boy for a seaman. Look how he stands there, sir, begging your pardon. Brave as a mast he is. Strong as pine . . ." How long Gabby would have continued Peter never found out for the captain cut him short.

"The sea," he roared, "is the eternal torment of mankind. 'Tis the curse of God from the days of the deluge, dividing nation from nation and brother from brother. 'Tis the end of hope and the threshold of hell. 'Tis the chastisement of sinners and—MR. WINTER, THAT FORETOPSAIL HALYARD LOOKS LIKE A WOMAN'S KNITTING WOOL. MAKE HER SNUG BRISTOL FASHION— the place where the wicked are purged. Do you hear the roaring of it now, boy? The deep growl and rumble of it? What makes that noise? 'Tis the bones of millions of men rolling on the floor of the ocean with every wave. We sail over the greatest graveyard in the world." He turned to Gabby.

"Sign him on for galley boy. Wages a shilling a week, all found."

"Aye, aye, sir," said Gabby.

"You'll like being galley boy," he said to Peter when they got below decks again. "Snug in the galley it is. Plenty of food. You won't forget to slip old Gabby a nice piece of fat bacon—just a mite rancid—when you gets a chance, will ye? I likes a nice piece of fat bacon, particularly if it's just a touch rancid. Not too much though. Fresh it's too rich for me stomach."

Peter did not like being galley boy, though. The cook was a tall, thin, melancholy individual utterly broken by years of attempting to keep fires lit at sea and food hot, and always criticized by the crew for, whatever their troubles, they concentrated their anger on the cook and his food.

His name was Hoyle, but since there was not an h to be found in the whole ship's company, he was called " 'Oyle" and this added to his torments, it being a common complaint that he put too much of his name in the food he served.

The bane of this unfortunate man's existence was the galley stove, a rusting iron box which, by some terrible piece of ill design, was so close to the floor that the elongated Hoyle spent all his working hours bent at the waist. It was as if he was constantly making obeisance to the frightful god or devil of a stove which he served.

The stove was fueled with blocks of wood, most of them pine and all of them green. In addition to being green, they were invariably damp so that to get the stove lit was the work of at least one blasphemous hour on the part of Hoyle. Of paper he had none so he had to content himself with wood shavings which he cut off the logs with a seaman's knife. These wood chips he baptized gingerly with a little fat and lit with a taper, fire being obtained from a smoky lantern which was always kept burning in the galley.

Once the fire was lit, it was but the start of the troubles

of the two. The stove was equipped with a tin flue on which time and the violence of shipboard life had worked a terrible havoc. It was bent, twisted, rusted and pierced in so many places and in so many ways that all it did was distribute the thick, black, lung-searing smoke from the green pine fire around the little galley.

Peter and Hoyle then worked in this smarting smoke-laden air, alternately going to the entryway and hanging their heads out to wipe the tears from their eyes and get a breath of fresh air.

It was, Peter discovered, a time-honored privilege of seamen to hang their soaking clothing in the galley where, though they would hardly dry in northern latitudes, they at least progressed from dripping wet to heavily damp.

So the cook and his helper in their tiny smoky quarters were surrounded by a cloakroom full of wet clothing. And often in these impossible circumstances, when the galley fire had been lit at last and a huge pot of potatoes had been put on it to boil, some pitch of the ship would send the pot crashing to the floor, scalding the two and frequently dousing the fire in the bargain.

When such things happened, Hoyle would strike out of the galley to the ship's rail and stand there like a statue, staring at the sea as if contemplating whether it would not be better to jump into it and end his miseries.

There were other troubles. One of them was taking the men's food to them in the forecastle. It was carried in a wooden bucket called a kip; potatoes, bacon, dried beans and the resulting greyish soup all in the same container.

To convey this safely across the rolling, slippery deck to the forecastle was no small feat. To get it to the forecastle still hot was all but impossible.

Quite often, in his early days as galley boy, Peter, to save himself in the pitching deck, dropped the kip and lost the men's meal. But he soon learned never to let go of the kip and, if it went overboard, he was made to understand that it was his job to go overboard with it; of the two, the kip was to be the first to be put back safely upon the deck.

The first two weeks, then, of life as a galley boy were all hardship. But they took Peter's mind off his troubles and, after a while, he began to enjoy himself.

The ship, he learned, was the *Maid of Malden*, a brig, and her owner was "Mr. John." Peter learned later that this "Mr. John" was Mr. John Hancock of Boston. Knowing nothing of the sea, it had never occurred to Peter that there was anything strange in the *Maid of Malden* starting a voyage from Boston in a howling gale. He thought that ships sailed whenever they were ready, and without reference to weather conditions.

"No," said Gabby, sucking on a rind of pork Peter had brought him, "most ships waits for wind and tide to favor them, and then they gets their clearances from the Customs House and the captain swears on oath that he is a loyal subject of the King and that he won't on no account do nothing at all that the King might have forbid somewhere or other.

"And then the port officer comes aboard and checks the cargo to see that it corresponds to what's in the ship's manifest. Then, of course, the port officer and the captain has a round of grog all around and meanwhile the hands is tramping around the capstan hauling up short until ordered to cease and things is got ready. And when the port officer has had his grog and got back into his boat, the captain he cocks an eye for the wind and calls for topsails and royals or whatever is right and . . ."

"Why did the *Maid of Malden* sail in a storm then?" asked Peter.

Gabby, who was seated in the forecastle on an upturned bucket, peered around in that gloomy enclosure as if he expected to see a King's officer hiding under one of the bunks.

"Because she's a free trader," said Gabby.

"And what's a free trader?" asked Peter.

"Oh, 'tis too much for yer poor head, boy," said Gabby, "and I don't know that I can rightly explain it, being a man that's not handy with words and accustomed to keeping me own counsel. That were a good piece o' bacon fat that were. Needs it to set me stomach right. Got to have it every day. Just a touch rancid. That's the way I likes it."

He reached in his ragged pocket and took out his roll of canvas with his quid of tobacco in it and cut himself off just the smallest piece.

"Ye don't chaw, do ye?" he said. He always asked this when he took out his tobacco in front of Peter.

"No," said Peter.

"Well, 'tis a nasty habit. But there's a power of comfort in it, particularly in a hard wind on a dark night. Makes a man feel that he ain't alone."

"What's a free trader?" Peter persisted.

"Lord, boy, but yer stubborn," said Gabby. "I gives a little touch to yer tiller, thinking ye'll come about on a new tack, but not you. You've got a long keel and are hard on the helmsman and holds to yer course and has to be brought about by backing yer jib and headsails generally."

Peter waited patiently.

"I'm long keeled meself," said Gabby. "Keel from stem to

transom one piece of wood. Don't chop and change around easy from one subject to another like most men do. Why, you start a conversation with some men and say maybe you're talking about loggerheads, and it ain't two minutes before they're telling you about something clean different like kidney pies. But that ain't the case with me. Holds to me course, I do. Like you."

Peter smiled. If there was one thing Gabby didn't do, it was hold to the subject under discussion.

"You still haven't told me what a free trader is," he said.

"Nope," said Gabby, "I didn't. Well, 'tis like this. Supposing you're in Boston and you're making, say, felt hats or maybe iron brackets or maybe boots. Boots is a good thing to make. I've often thought if ever I was to leave the sea I'd set meself up cobbling, for most people is partial to shoes and boots. You got to think of them kinds of things when you're planning your life. I knew a feller . . ." He caught Peter's eye, sighed and said, "So you're making felt hats or maybe boots. Boots is better. Now you wants to sell them boots and you ain't particular who buys them, whether he's a Frenchman or maybe a Dutchman—but they wears wood boots of their own so there ain't much market there—or maybe he might be a Spanish. It don't matter. So you starts to sell them and you got to ship them, see, to the French and the Turks—did I mention Turks before?—and so on.

"Now that's plain. But along comes the King in his parliament in England and the bootmakers in England goes up to the King, hat in hand, and says, 'Yer Majesty, there's a rascal there in Boston is selling boots to the French and being as there's only so many Frenchmen and each of them with but two legs, and likely a few hundred of them with but one, for they've fought many wars have the French, why he's cutting into our trade. Taking the bread out of our mouths, Yer Majesty, that are yer loyal and loving subjects and paid up our taxes handsomely and bought you that fine crown and them dandy clothes yer wearing.'

" 'Is that so?' says the King, taking a pinch out of a gold snuff box that he's picked up that morning while passing the Treasury, 'upon me word. We can't have that.'

" 'No,' says the bootmakers, ' 'tain't natural. 'Tain't what Providence had in mind and 'tis contrary to all the laws of Nature for boots to be made in Boston to be sold to the French. 'Twould be a merciful thing in keeping with Yer Majesty's wisdom and care for his subjects if you did decree that nobody was to make boots in Boston and sell them to the French.'

" 'I've got a better idea,' said the King. 'Let them make the boots and send them to London here in English ships and we'll sell them to the French. That way you gentlemen don't have to make any boots at all but you can still get your profit selling the Boston boots. And the ship masters of England will make a profit carrying them. They was here this morning complaining that trade is poorly and I promised to do what I could for them.'

" 'Your Majesty is right as always,' says the bootmakers.

" 'Have a pinch of snuff, gentlemen,' says the King. And there it is.

"You, making your boots in Boston, finds you can't sell them to the French no more, but has to pay passage for them on an English ship and sell them to the London bootmakers at a reduced price, so they can sell them to the French. And soon there isn't a penny profit in it and you give up making boots and haven't any work to do. For what goes for boots, goes for felt hats and iron brackets and women's corsets and wagon wheels and doors and window frames and everything.

"So there's no work in Boston and short rations for all hands. That's what's called 'unfree trade' or sometimes lawyers calls it 'restraint of trade,' lawyers being fancy."

That gave Peter something to think about. Was this the reason why there was the mob in Boston—the ever-present mob of ragged, hungry, homeless and desperate men? He had always heard from his father that they were ne'er-do-wells and idlers who wouldn't work. But now it looked as though the King and the bootmakers of England—and all the other makers of a thousand other articles—were determined that there never would be work for the Boston men to do—and the men in all the other cities of the colonies.

And was this the reason why Mr. Fielding could make only barrel staves and not barrels?

"Free trade," said Gabby, interrupting his thoughts, "is just the opposite of unfree trade. In free trade you takes no notice of what the King agreed with the bootmakers, but just goes ahead and sells your goods anyway."

"But that's breaking the law," said Peter, aghast.

"It is," said Gabby. "But I'm not a man to get involved with the law. It muddles me head something awful, like that alphabet with them letters that sounds alike but are as different as knighthead and ruddle pintle. What you got to look out for, young feller, is to do what's sensible and never mind the law."

"But supposing that what's sensible is contrary to the law?" asked Peter.

"Then heave the law overboard, books, seals, wigs, whereases and all the rest of that tackle," said Gabby.

"Wouldn't that be revolution?" asked Peter.

"It would," said Gabby. "I 'ear 'Oyle shouting for you so maybe he's put the fire out again. I do believe that man would be safe in Hell, for he's a natural enemy to fire is 'Oyle."

Hoyle had indeed managed to put out the galley fire and Peter set to work to relight it while Hoyle sulked and complained and made it appear that it was entirely the boy's fault that the fire had gone out, for he had not been there to attend to it.

But Peter bore this patiently and thought about what Gabby had said about free traders. He smiled over the picture of the bootmakers and the King. Yet he concluded that something of this sort might well be happening, and it was beyond argument that the manufacturers of England were nearer to the parliament and the throne than the manufacturers of the struggling colonies on the American continent.

Gabby's talk aroused Peter's curiosity about what kind of cargo the *Maid of Malden* was carrying to the French West Indies for Mr. John Hancock of Boston. He soon learned.

There were barrels of salted cod and dried peas and flour and, added to these, bales of woolen stockings and felt hats and kegs of nails and iron bolts and, deep down in the hold, twenty tons of iron sheets of different sizes. It all sounded very dull and Peter said so plainly to Gabby.

"What was you expecting?" asked Gabby. "Peacocks' feathers maybe, and ivory tusks and blue velvet cloths all pricked out with gold lace? What you've got to bear in mind is that we shouldn't be carrying as much as a tenpenny nail unless we was shipping it direct to Bristol or London. And if we're stopped by a British war vessel, we're for it."

"What would happen?" asked Peter.

"Maybe you'll find out," said Gabby, taciturn for once, "and maybe you won't."

Chapter 8

THE GLOOM and anger of the New England seas were within a week replaced by the sparkling blue of tropical water as the *Maid of Malden* lumbered southward with her commonplace but illegal cargo.

Captain Pleashed, who while his vessel was near the American coast had hardly left the quarterdeck, now took to his cabin, a sign that danger from both the weather and the British naval patrol was past for the present. His mates took over the direction of the ship, led by the first mate, Mr. Winter, a sober, patient, grey-haired man who bore up under the tempests of the ocean and the tempests of his sea-hating captain with the greatest composure.

He had, Gabby said, been at sea ever since he was Peter's age and, in marked contrast to the captain, loved the sea so much that he could hardly be persuaded to go ashore even when the vessel lay two or three weeks in port.

The *Maid* did not take a direct course to the French Indies, as they were called, but stood out to sea both to clear the American coast and the naval patrol. She was a thousand miles out in the Atlantic before she put about to head for the

French island. And at all times a lookout was posted in her main topmast—even at dead of night—and any time a sail was sighted, the helmsman altered course to avoid contact and recognition.

It took them five weeks before the vessel was off the French island at Martinique, and in that time conditions aboard had much improved. As soon as the ship reached warmer latitudes, the sailors stowed their stormy weather gear so that the tiny galley was no longer a cloakroom crowded with dripping clothing.

Now it was easier to get clothes dried by hanging them on lines strung from the standing rigging. Soon the *Maid of Malden* looked like a Boston backyard on a washday. All kinds of clothing were hung up on these lines to give them an airing and prevent mildew and one day Peter was surprised to find the captain's strange turban hung from a line. He would dearly have liked to see Captain Pleashed without his headgear. While the turban was drying out, the captain remained in his cabin, his meals taken to him by Hoyle, and Peter's curiosity about the captain's head increased more and more.

"What kind of a head has the captain got?" he asked Hoyle one day.

"Same like you and me," said Hoyle. And then he added, "Only different."

"How is it different?"

"He were scalped," said Hoyle. It was a warm day and the galley fire was going well, so Hoyle was in a communicative mood.

"Scalped," he repeated. "Ain't got nothing over his skull but a little weak kind of skin that's mostly scabs and sores. You know anything about scalping?"

"Yes," said Peter, "the Indians do it. I thought they only took a little piece of the forelock, though, for a trophy."

"That's what they used ter do," said Hoyle. "Until there was a bounty put on scalps by the English during the wars. Then one brave would take one piece, see, that being worth five shillings in tobacco, and then another took another piece, and so on until if a feller fell into their hands, why they took his whole scalp off.

"And those heathens didn't mind whether it was a Frenchman they was scalping or an Englishman. Every piece of hair was worth five shillings in tobacco. Captain, he fell into their hands and so he lost his whole scalp and lucky to come out alive.

"Left his head mighty tender, which is why he can't stand it to be cold, nor rained on, nor snowed on, nor the sun to shine on it. That's how come he made that there turban—for protection, see, for his tender head."

"Wouldn't a good wig have done?" asked Peter.

"No," snapped Hoyle. "You ever heard of anybody water-proofing a wig? Besides, wigs gets full of vermin on board a ship."

"Does Captain Pleashed really hate the sea as much as he says?" asked Peter.

"More," said Hoyle. " 'ates it almost as much as I do."

"Why do you stay at sea since you dislike the life?" asked Peter.

"You're bothering my 'ead with all these questions," said Hoyle. " 'ow do I know? I ain't never thought of it. I just 'ate it, that's all."

Peter found that most of the sailors on the *Maid* were great sea-haters. Yet in their leisure hours in fine weather, they built model boats or made fancy knots in ropes—they had a wonderful variety of names for these knots—or talked of ships they'd been on or captains they'd sailed under. And much as they maintained they disliked the sea, they were downright afraid of the land and, when ashore, lived as close to the waterfront as they might.

"I starts getting anxious just as soon as I gets ashore," one of them told Peter. " 'tis the noise, I think. All them shrill-voiced women around. And them carts rumbling and bumping down the road and the carters cracking their whips. And it don't smell good ashore. Mostly it smells like slops and sewage. Land's a dirty place. Look how it fouls up the water in the harbors."

This man undertook with Gabby to teach Peter the names of the sails, ropes and masts which formed the rigging of the *Maid*. The variety was utterly bewildering.

There were braces and bowlines and backstays and mainstays and topmast shrouds.

There were foot ropes and sheets and halyards and downhauls.

There were belaying pins and parrals and clew lines and reef points and ratlines. And all these were but the main headings of much of the rigging, for halyards could be peak or throat for one sail—the driver or spanker—but main topsail, or main topgallant or fore royal and so on for the others.

Each of these ropes was fastened or "belayed" in a particular place and only in that place on a belaying pin. To belay it anywhere else, whatever the hurry, was the gravest offense. Sails might have to be reefed or clewed up or taken down in a howling gale at dead of night. The crew didn't need to see the necessary line. They could put their hands on them in the dark, since they were always belayed on the same belaying pins. Slipshod belaying of a sheet or halyard could wreck a vessel on such an occasion.

Peter never thought he'd learn to make order out of all this mass of rope. But Gabby and the other seaman, a man called Small John, undertook to teach him. In return for this, Peter agreed to teach the two of them the alphabet.

"Fore royal halyard," Gabby would shout and Peter was expected to go immediately to the particular pin on which it was belayed. In return he would ask, "What comes after *m*?" and Gabby would scratch his head with clawlike fingers, roll his quid of tobacco around in his mouth and mutter and struggle with this appalling problem in literacy. Peter indeed made faster progress with sailoring than his two seaman pupils did with letters until he hit upon an idea.

He gave to each piece of the rigging the name of a letter of the alphabet. The main halyard became *a*, the mainbrace *b*, the main royal halyard *c* and so on. And then the alphabet finally made sense to the two men and they would recite it one to the other, in front of their mates, with a remarkable air of superiority.

Hoyle didn't approve of this. "Book learning," he said, " 'ain't for seamen. When seamen can read, like the captain, who's going ter be captain?"

Two hundred miles off Martinique at dawn one day, the lookout hailed the deck to report a sail. Mr. Winter ordered the helmsman to alter course away from it and the sail was soon lost below the horizon. But half an hour later another sail was reported and course had to be altered again. Mr. Winter reported the two ships to the captain, who came on deck.

"Sail still in sight?" the captain shouted to the lookout through a speaking trumpet.

"Aye, sir," cried the lookout, "coming up hard on our

larboard beam."

"What do you make of her?" roared Captain Pleashed.

The lookout examined the vessel through his telescope for some seconds.

" 'Tain't an Indiaman," he said.

This information, of so negative a nature, threw the captain immediately into a rage.

"Blind your wormy eyes!" he roared. "What kind of report is that? 'Tain't an Indiaman! I don't want to know what it ain't but what it is. Mr. Winter, send someone aloft that's got eyes in his head instead of rotted turnips."

Another man, at a word from the mate, sped up the rigging to the lookout and soon he was reporting to the deck.

"Deck ho," he shouted. "Looks like a frigate."

"Stand by to 'ware ship," roared Captain Pleashed on receiving this information.

"Hands to sheets and braces," snapped Mr. Winter, and then to the helmsman, "Down helm, mister."

The *Maid* slewed around before the wind to run from the strange frigate, her loosened sails bellying out from their yards. Sailing before the wind, all was much quieter aboard the brig. But the lessening of the noises of the wind and the sea was made up for to no small extent by Captain Pleashed who, in a sweat of anxiety, roared a stream of curses at the ocean, the sky, the brig and the pursuing frigate. He calmed down enough for a moment to hail the lookout again and demand whether he could see what colors the frigate flew.

"British colors, sir," said the lookout.

This brought another torrent of abuse from the captain against all things British from the British King to the British Navy and all through the British Navy from Admirals to bosuns. He had an astonishing talent for this sort of invective and had arrived at the point when he was cursing the kinds of ships of the British Navy, from first-raters to sloops of war, when he suddenly stopped.

"Mr. Winter," he said, "heave to and run up French colors." The captain, unable to show a clean pair of heels to the frigate, had decided to take a double gamble.

He hoped that flying French colors, he might be let go without inspection, for the British at the time were wary of boarding French merchantmen on the high seas, though this was not to be relied upon. And there was a slim chance, being so close to Martinique, that the frigate was not British at all but a Frenchman flying British colors—this being a common practice of the day.

Round came the *Maid* into the wind, her mainsail clewed up and her main yards backed. The frigate flew down upon her like a hawk upon a pigeon, circled around her stern, and came up on the weather side and likewise hove to.

"What ship are you?" roared a lieutenant, standing in the mainmast shrouds.

"*Français*, blast your eyes," roared back Captain Pleashed, so angered that he forgot in his reply to keep up the disguise of being French. Peter could see the grin on the lieutenant's bronzed face, at the reply.

"What port of France—Boston?" shouted the lieutenant and across the water came a roar of laughter from the crew of the frigate.

"I'm sending a boat over," the lieutenant continued. "Have your papers ready."

"Send a boat if you wish," shouted Captain Pleashed, "but send a surgeon with it. I've got Yellow Jack aboard. Half my crew's down with it."

The lieutenant hesitated. Yellow Jack was the dread

of seamen; a tropical fever whose origin was unknown at the time. It struck so savagely that healthy men had been known to drop down from it as if felled by a pole ax and die within the hour. It was, furthermore, a disease rampant in the French West Indian Islands though common in all tropical ports, and highly contagious.

"By thunder," said the lieutenant at length, "I think you're lying."

"By thunder," said Captain Pleashed, "if you had the hardihood of a maggot, you'd send a boat over and find out." He added, in a whisper to Winter, "Get ten of the sickest-looking men aboard in their bunks, wet them down with bilge water so that they look like they're sweating and see that they smell. Have Nobby pull his skylark."

The lieutenant did not quite know what to do about this blunt challenge and was joined now by the captain. A consultation took place between the two of them, and finally the lieutenant shouted:

"I'm not coming aboard. I'm sending a boat. Lower your papers into it and keep to windward of me."

"I'll lower no papers of mine into your lousy bumboat," roared Captain Pleashed. "You inspect my papers aboard my ship or not at all." He suddenly recalled that he was supposed to be French and added, *"Sacre bleu."*

"You'll do as I say or I'll sink you," shouted the lieutenant.

"Sink me and be sorry," cried Captain Pleashed. "Sink me and take the consequence of sinking a peaceful French merchantman."

"You're bold enough man to be from Boston," said the lieutenant.

"I'm bold enough man to stand up to any King's ship,"

said Pleashed.

"Lower that boat," cried the lieutenant, now white with anger.

But at that moment, a man came bursting out of the forecastle of the *Maid*, prompted, Peter found out later, by the mate, for this was an old ruse of Captain Pleashed's. He plunged across the deck, tearing at his clothes, and, at the sight of him, the crew of the brig scattered like dry leaves before a puff of wind, leaping to the bulwarks and into the rigging and climbing upward to be away from their ship-mate. The man reached the foot of the mainmast and there collapsed and lay moaning on the deck.

The men of the British frigate were just lowering a boat as ordered and had it swung overboard on the davits when this strange performance occurred on the deck of the brig. They hesitated, there was another conference between the lieutenant and his captain and Captain Pleashed shouted, "Send a surgeon for the love of God or we're all dead men aboard here."

That did it. A kind of panic gripped the British vessel. The boat was swung inboard again. The yards were trimmed to the wind and the frigate sheered off without another word. Captain Pleashed watched it go and then returned to his cabin, and the *Maid* resumed her course for Martinique.

But her troubles were not over yet. Shortly after mid-day, they fell in with another British vessel, for the British naval patrol off the French islands, designed to prevent the American colonies trading with them, was heavy. The second British ship was a sloop of war and, though Captain Pleashed tried the same ruse as he had used on the frigate, this time his luck had run out.

"Come aboard if you wish," yelled Captain Pleashed

when the two vessels were hove to, "but send a surgeon for half my crew is down with Yellow Jack." It was as if he were reading a part from a play and the "fever men" were already in their bunks, ready for their second wetting of the day with bilge water.

"You're the unluckiest ship for Yellow Jack I ever came across," replied the Britisher.

"What do you mean?" spluttered Captain Pleashed.

"I mean," said the officer, "that when I commanded the *Centaur* but three months ago, you had Yellow Jack then. It seems that Yellow Jack must be a member of your crew. Stand by to receive my boat and have your papers ready, you Boston rebel. I have you this time."

"No you haven't, by thunder," said Captain Pleashed, "lower that boat and I'll fire into you."

The threat was not idle, for the Maid mounted six four-pounders, four on her poop and two on the forecastle head. It was a common enough practice for merchant vessels which frequently had to defend themselves, particularly in voyages off the European coast where the Barbary pirates ranged all the way from the English Channel to the African Bight of Benin. The *Maid* not infrequently cruised to Europe and to Africa.

"Fire on a King's ship and I'll have you hanged for a rebel and a pirate," cried the Britisher.

"Load with round shot," the captain barked and the crew of the *Maid* ran back the little guns, charged and loaded them and ran them forward.

The Britisher lowered his boat and as it hit the water there was a high crack from the guns of the *Maid*. A puff of white powder smoke wreathed up the side of the brig and dissipated slowly over the deck. But hardly had the report died away before the sloop of war opened fire and her shot smacked into the side of the *Maid*, sending the splinters flying up into the air.

Peter was astounded. Here was open war between a British merchantman and a British naval vessel. But he had not time to think for suddenly it seemed that pieces of the deck of the *Maid* were being ripped up, and something hummed past his head like an angry bee. Marines on the sloop of war, standing in the rigging, were firing down on the deck of the *Maid*.

"Square away," barked Captain Pleashed to the helmsman and the brig swung around to present her stern to the enemy.

Placed before the wind, she quickly drew away, for the sloop of war was hove to and taken by surprise at the audacity of the merchantman. The distance between the two vessels widened rapidly and then there came a shout of delight from the crew of the *Maid*. Peter saw the foremast of the sloop of war topple, the result of a lucky shot from the brig.

But in the next second the main topmast of the *Maid* was splintered off just above the truck and toppled down to be caught in the rigging and swing there, a useless tatter of canvas, rope and timber.

The two ships now limped after each other, firing whenever there was an opportunity. But the *Maid* gradually pulled out of gunshot and toward sunset the sloop of war sheered off, for they were now in French territorial waters.

Peter was convinced that there would be a heavy price to be paid one day by Captain Pleashed and all aboard the *Maid* for opening fire on the British sloop of war. And Gabby agreed with him, adding that the price would be paid only if they were caught.

"But," he said, "bear this in mind. 'Tain't only this brig that has trouble with the British. 'Tis every ship that sails from an American port. We must either rebel and fight or there is an end to all American shipping and to all American trade, which ain't a natural state of affairs at all.

"There ain't a lobster boat puts out from an American port that can't be stopped and searched by them Britishers. Aye, and many of the men pressed into service aboard British ships and that within sight of their own homes.

"Things'll come to blows one day in earnest. This is but sparring. But come to blows it will, like I said, with the shot flying and the muskets rattling and people crying for the King and people crying for the colonies and what will be the end of it, no man can say. Not even Mr. John."

"You mean Mr. Hancock," said Peter.

"I said Mr. John," replied Gabby.

Chapter 9

THE *MAID OF MALDEN* stayed three weeks at Fort de France, the principal city of the island of Martinique, unloading her cargo and taking on, in exchange for it, fifteen hundred barrels of molasses. There were two other American vessels in the harbor, "free traders" like the *Maid*, and the island was soon buzzing with news of the engagement of the *Maid* with the British sloop.

Captain Pleashed was immediately in trouble when he got ashore, for it was soon known that he had flown French colors during the engagement. The French authorities, led by the governor, fearful that this might lead to an outbreak of war between Britain and France, were for handing the brig, its captain and crew over to the British.

They were prevented from taking this action by the merchants of the city, all of them hot against the British, for their trade was much crippled by the British naval patrol of the island. Nonetheless, two days after the *Maid* docked, a platoon of French soldiers marched down to the wharf, very neat in their blue coats and white knee breeches, with orders to board the *Maid*, seize her captain and crew, and confine them to prison. But Captain Pleashed cared as little for French grenadiers as he did for a British sloop of war.

"Load them cannon," he ordered and the guns were loaded and trained on the platoon of soldiers.

"Now then, you confounded frogs," roared the captain, "board a British ship here on a peaceful trading mission, and I'll smash you all to kingdom come." It was then that the merchants of Fort de France took a hand. A huge crowd had collected around the soldiers, remarkably like the mob that could collect in an instant in the streets of Boston in this century of mobs. They carried cudgels and stones and, egged on by the merchants, started to shout and throw stones at the soldiers just as the Boston mob had stoned the Redcoats many a time. It was all very strange to Peter, for it seemed that all over the world civilians hated soldiers and mobs were intent upon taking over control of affairs.

The soldiers dodged and swore but the hail of stones only increased and eventually their captain, between the guns of the *Maid* and the brickbats of the mob, marched his men in considerable disorder back to their barracks.

But that was only the beginning of the matter. The mob had not yet had as much sport as was desired, so it streamed off now to the governor's mansion, flung its stones through the windows, stormed over his gardens uprooting shrubs and trampling down flowers and eventually breaking into the mansion, seized the unfortunate governor and brought him down to the harbor. They threw him into the water. Nor was he allowed to climb ashore again until he had promised that no action would be taken against the *Maid*.

So the ship discharged its cargo and took aboard its barrels of molasses; when this was done, the crew was allowed a day ashore.

Peter went with Gabby into a city which was a strange mixture of filth and beauty. Flowers abounded on every side—the flaming scarlet of hibiscus contrasting with the snow white of lilies and the sulphur yellow of other waxy flowers whose name Peter did not know.

There was a multitude of birds: tiny hummingbirds that darted like jeweled bees from blossom to blossom, and blue and yellow parrots which whirled in flocks over the roofs like so many pigeons. Ferns, he found, grew to a height of ten feet and sprang out from every fissure in the rocks or between the stone of walls and houses.

But side by side with this were the squalid streets with sewage flowing down the middle of them, and garbage left to rot in alleyways. Over this garbage big bare-necked vultures fought wary duels with dogs whose hunched spines and gaunt ribs spoke of starvation.

Behind the city, the cool verdure-clad mountains rose up until their tops were swathed in a shimmering silver mist. But in the streets was all the ugliness that disease and poverty could produce. Men with limbs swollen beyond belief from elephantiasis squatted in the shade of palm trees begging or selling bruised fruit thick with flies. Others, like bundles of rags, slept in the shade, waiting for nothing that Peter could think of but death. There was an air of crushing hopelessness over the city, despite the beauty of the flowers and the mountains and the birds, so that Peter got the impression that Fort de France was Paradise converted into Hell.

He soon got tired of walking around and with Gabby went back to the harbor.

The *Maid of Malden* sailed from Martinique by dark as she

had sailed from Boston by dark. She eased her way out of the harbor in a light wind, without benefit of pilots, relying on her lookouts to stay clear of the coral reefs—seen as a shimmer of phosphorescence on the surface of the somber water.

Once clear of the tricky harbor entrance, she plunged into the darkness of the ocean, all sails set, like a thief hurrying home with his booty. Captain Pleashed had chosen a moonless night for his departure to evade the British watch on the island, and once again he set a course deep into the Atlantic before heading north and west for his home port.

At dawn the *Maid* was a hundred miles out to sea. With the coming of the next dawn, they were three hundred miles deep into the Atlantic, and then for a day the wind which had been steady from the west dropped completely. The brig rolled and dipped and wallowed in a disturbed sea, the waves seeming to come from every quarter. The ship's rigging hummed and jerked under these unusual stresses, her timbers creaked. Below decks there was an uneasy and ominous groaning as the brig's big ribs worked under the strain.

Peter watched the waves, clinging to the mainmast backstay, and analyzed their movement. From the northeast came a steady succession of giant rollers, spaced thirty feet apart and each of them about twelve feet from crest to trough. From the west came smaller yet steeper-sided waves, slapping into these rollers, creaming over their ridges, spilling into the troughs between them, and then re-forming to continue their strange conflict. Such a motion puzzled him, for he had always thought that waves could come from only one direction at a time.

"The smaller waves," said Gabby, "are from the west

wind we 'ad from Martinique. The big uns, they're from some storm over to the east and north." He glanced up at the steel blue and oddly menacing sky in which the merest slivers of white cloud, elongated and jagged as splinters, were beginning to form.

"Better tell that 'Oyle ter lash everything he's got in the galley so it can't move," he said. "We're in for hurricane weather. Maybe an hour and maybe two hours, but 'twill be here as sure as death."

Hoyle received the message gloomily, as indeed he received all messages, and Peter helped get everything safely stowed in the galley.

"If it's a 'urricane coming up," said Hoyle, "you'd best report to Mr. Winter. They'll need all hands in a 'urricane."

While Peter had been busy in the galley, the men had been busy about the decks. Hatches were double battened and boats double lashed. All sails were taken in except for a rag of a fore topsail and one staysail and these were of double canvas and sheeted home not with ropes but with chain—in itself a grim enough circumstance. Three men were working the pumps aft, getting the last drop of water out of the bilges, for there would be work enough ahead without starting with water aboard. And the bosun had prepared a number of bags soaked with oil which, lowered over the side when the hurricane struck, would help to lessen the seas in the immediate vicinity of the ship.

Now the crew stood around in groups and, despite the sultry heat of the sun, many of them already wore their rough-weather gear. They were nervous and tense and there was no conversation or skylarking among them. They glanced up at the rigging and spars and over the sides at the sea and looked at the scud of cloud thickening overhead and stared over the dazzling bright, confused ocean to the northeastern horizon.

"Your eyes good?" Mr. Winter asked when Peter reported to him.

"Yes, sir," Peter replied.

"Get up to the fore topmast and hail the deck when you see the wind."

"How shall I know it when I see it?" asked Peter.

"You'll know it," said the mate grimly.

Peter went up the pitching, jerking rigging which, like a horse with an unwanted rider, seemed intent upon throwing him off. One second the ratlines would be loose in his hands and under his feet. The next second they would become as rigid as iron bars snapped taut by the pitching and rolling of the brig. The motion was not merely a roll from side to side, but a jerking at the same time fore and aft and none of these movements were coordinated. The pitching up or down often came in the middle of a deep sideways swoop and the boy's hands and arms ached with fatigue before he was able to gain his lookout post.

Here, sixty feet above the deck, all movements were exaggerated and Peter was unable to do more than cling to the slim foretopmast for several minutes until he could, after much struggling and many terrors, lash himself to the mast. Then still, he looked around at the glittering and wild ocean.

All, from horizon to horizon, was of a scintillating and confused brightness. The ocean seemed in a panic, the opposing waves running into each other sometimes with a hiss like steam escaping and sometimes with a sharp crack like cannon shot. The effect was like a crowd of people expecting some catastrophe and running in every direction, uncertain of where safety lay. Splashes of white exploded without warning into the air. Big blue shoulders of water raised themselves up out of the ocean and came crashing down upon their base, the white foam colliding with the sharper fierce waves running from the west, so that at times as much as an acre of the ocean was a cauldron of foam.

And still the air was quiet. Not a puff of wind stirred. The ship groaned and creaked, the rigging jerked, the two sails flapped. The brig waited.

Then, far away to the northeast a dirty rim of black, like a fingernail, appeared on the horizon. It spread rapidly, pushing the blue confused, panicked seas before it. It was like a growth, feeding and multiplying upon itself, and this growth spread not only outward over the ocean but upward into the sky. This was the wind coming like a wall upon them, the blackness growing wider and higher with each second.

"Deck ho," yelled Peter and pointed. "Wind," he yelled.

"Come down," yelled the mate. "Lively."

By the time the boy had unlashed himself, he felt just the slightest puff or two of wind on his cheek. He would not have noticed it on a summer's day, but now this merest touch of air filled him with fear. From behind him, over to the northeast, he heard a slight whimper, scarcely to be picked out above the ship noises. And yet, tiny as a mouse's cry, it was the very voice of menace. The air stirred impatiently around him and the whimpering increased in intensity and then the boy picked out a deeper note, a sullen roar, and glanced behind him. One-third of the ocean and sky now was black, the waters not to be distinguished from the air above them. Through this blackness came jagged rips of lightning so far off that they looked but an inch in size. Streaks of bone white appeared in the blackness of the sea and the roaring increased with every second.

"Down," yelled Gabby, standing by the foremast backstay. "Down now, for your life."

Suddenly the boy was flung against the rigging as the ship heeled viciously over. A puff of wind screamed past and smote the sea beyond the ship, ripping the tops off the waves and sending the foam scattered like grapeshot over their surface. The mouse whimper of the storm had gone but was replaced by a howling that rose and fell like the hunting cry of a wolf pack. A scattering of rain in heavy, long white streaks flew through the rigging and the ship righted itself, yawing violently toward the storm.

The boy took one more terrified look behind him and saw the black fury of the storm rushing down on the brig. Out of it came a monstrous roar and before it rode a cauldron of foam. This came nearer and nearer and with each second the roaring increased. Peter felt his lungs so heavy in his chest that he seemed unable to get his breath. The sky had now completely clouded over and gusts of wind, as solid as barn doors, it seemed, were flinging down upon the brig.

He grabbed the foretop gallant halyard, crossed his legs around it and came sliding to the deck.

As he reached the deck the cauldron of white water before the storm reached the brig. She spun crazily around, turned broadside, wallowed in a trough of the sea, heeled over, and managed to get her stern to the storm.

And then, when she had done this, the wind struck.

Chapter 10

THE WIND carried with it noise and darkness and furious motion. It was the very soul of fury and struck the *Maid of Malden* with the impact of cannon shot. The little brig shuddered and seemed to sink down in the water under the force of the blow. She buried her bows in a smother of sea and over her stern came a wash of foam which obliterated her decks so that Peter, still clinging to the halyard, was buried to the neck in this welter. His feet were dragged from under him, his grasp of the halyard all but torn loose.

He struggled for breath and found no breath, but still held on grimly, held on as if the halyard was his life and if he let go he would surely die.

And then the little brig, slowly and wearily but doggedly, clawed her way upward out of the foam. The top of her poop rail appeared, then the deadeyes of her mainstays, then the starboard rail and finally she was free of the ocean, which in the first impact of the hurricane had all but pulled her down.

But this relief was but momentary. There was a boiling mass of water up forward, rushing toward the forecastle, exploding against hatch covers, pin rails and the capstan, and this had not cleared the deck before the boy saw a vast dark mountain rise behind the ship.

Higher and higher this mass of water raised itself until it seemed to be as high as the mainmast. The top of it was a streaming white, as when fog is being stripped from the peak of a mountain. The sides gleamed dully in the gloom and down these sides came cascades of roaring water, its roar heard above the shrieking and piping of the wind in the rigging.

It seemed to the boy that this mountain of a wave must sweep over the ship, smashing it to pieces and drowning or tearing it apart in its fury. He caught a glimpse of the three men at the wheel aft, peering back as a monster bore down upon them. It was their task to keep the ship's stern to this sea. If she broached—turned broadside to it—she would be rolled over and over like a barrel plunging down a hill.

There was a minute when the brig seemed to be held in the water as if the seas had turned to glue. Then her forward motion seemed to be reversed and she drove backward toward the monstrous wave, sucked into it as though the wave were hungry to devour the vessel. Then, stern first, the brig rolled up the pursuing wave; up the monstrous sides with the water hissing and cascading past them. Higher and higher she went and when she had almost reached the top, the wave, lashed by the screaming wind, burst over the vessel.

Again the decks of the brig disappeared; again the boiling water left only her two masts above them. The seas went over Peter's head and once more he was swept off his feet and felt himself being dragged away from the halyard, which was his only lifeline. Then the crest passed and the *Maid* rose out of the smother.

But this time Peter did not wait. Made a plaything by the wind, he scrambled and stumbled, falling, filled with terror, for the break of the poop, flung open a companionway door and plunged below. There, in utter blackness, he felt the *Maid* rise to another wave, and groped his way forward between decks to the forecastle.

The crew, Gabby among them, had already sought cover and were crowded in the forecastle in their bunks, still in their oilskins and seaboots. There was no talking. In the thundering roar around the ship, in the screaming of the wind overhead, in the deep hum of the rigging, transmitted into the forecastle by the vibrating mast, a shout would have been as ineffective as a whisper.

There was a rope along the inside of Peter's bunk and he had to loop an arm through this to prevent himself being pitched to the deck. Water flooded into the forecastle from above through the hatch which, though battened down, still was not watertight. The sea came in in sheets as each roller swept the vessel and the men looked at it grimly and thought of the water which must be collecting in the cargo hold amidships and aft.

The noise in the forecastle was even worse and more terrifying than it had been on deck. Each time the brig buried her nose in the sea, the whole forecastle shook as if it would be crushed. The impact was as if the ship had driven onto a rock. There would be a heavy "boom" and then the groan of the timbers and all the time the sound of cascading waters outside and above that of the shrieking of the wind.

The mast fascinated Peter. It passed through the deck into the forecastle and through the forecastle deck to the keel. The section which showed in the forecastle was twelve or fourteen inches thick. Yet it trembled like a reed in a swift-flowing river, and rocked from side to side as if it must tear out the two decks through which it passed.

For ten hours the hurricane raged, its force undiminished. The men at the wheel were relieved every hour and those who returned when their trick was up were so exhausted that their mates had to help them into their bunks and lash them there.

Peter saw the hands of some of these men who had stood a trick at the wheel. They were black with cold, the fingers blue and swollen and the palms bloodied from being stripped of skin. When Gabby returned from his trick, his face was as grey as wood ash and his hands so battered that Peter knowing his needs, volunteered to cut him a chaw of tobacco, for the old seaman was incapable of performing the task himself.

Gabby put the chaw in his mouth and, when Peter next looked at him, Gabby was fast asleep, lashed into his bunk and pitching and rolling, but unconscious of it all.

Peter wished heartily that he could sleep, but he could not. He could not even think in the pandemonium and noise, and every part of him ached. He was confused as much by the noise as by the wild destructive motion, and at each second expected the brig to founder.

The hurricane had struck in the midafternoon. By midnight the water in the forecastle was up to the lower bunks and the bosun's head appeared briefly in the companionway with a yell of which Peter caught only the word "hands."

The men tumbled from their bunks and fought themselves into the outer fury. Peter followed. In the pitch black, nothing could be seen of the sea around. The ship pitched and tossed in a howling blackness. The men clinging to lifelines, rigged before the hurricane broke, floundered to the pumps. They knew, without hearing the order, what was expected of them. The pumps were located aft near the break of the poop where there was some slight shelter from the weather. They were operated by seesaw levers and had already been rigged. The men worked at them for two hours in the howling, tearing wind, with the seas breaking over them and sweeping them from their feet. Peter helped with the work, not out of a sense of duty but out of a sense of fear that if he withheld even his own small efforts, the ship would surely founder.

At the end of the two hours, the hurricane showed signs of abating. The wind moderated to gale force, and then there would be intervals of perhaps ten seconds when there would be no wind at all, though the seas were as high and roaring as ever. And then there came a time when the wind had gone completely and the waves, though mountainous, no longer were slashed with streaks of steaming foam.

"Is it over?" Peter asked.

"No," said Gabby. "We're in the eye of it—a quiet place in the middle of the storm. 'Tis always like this.

"Twenty minutes this will last, more or less. Maybe twenty-two. I were in a storm off the Celebes where the quiet part lasted upward of an hour but then we had a Dutch captain and they do say Dutchmen are lucky, one having given his soul to the devil so that his mates could survive the storm. That's what they say though I don't know whether 'tis true. But in the middle of that storm off the Celebes, we had a full hour and could pump out almost dry. But for us, twenty minutes. Maybe twenty-five."

The pumps went on with their clang-clang-clang, during the windless period. Then the winds started again, sharp, vicious blasts screaming out of the darkness and leaping on the brig and sending her staggering and heeling over in the sea. Then once more came the piping and shrilling and roaring and the waves boiled aboard, sweeping the decks from stem to stern. The wind had now changed direction. It had been from the northeast but now raged from the southwest, and it seemed to Peter that it blew even harder than before.

Work at the pumps was soon impossible. Then men scrambled below and got back to the forecastle, and tumbled exhausted into their soaking bunks. An hour before dawn the hurricane had reached a pitch never before touched. This was evident by the heavier vibration of the mast and the drumming of the stays, transmitted through the ship's planking, and by the higher shriek of the wind. Suddenly the whole ship shook and the foremast which had been banging back and forth and from side to side now thundered and rocked with demonic vigor.

"Mainstay's parted," someone shouted.

There was no need for all hands to be summoned. The men leaped from their bunks and plunged up to the deck. There they found the foremast swaying wildly in increasing arcs. The larboard shrouds had parted and the mast no longer received the support needed to hold it erect.

"Bring her down," roared Mr. Winter through his trumpet. Two of the men seized axes and hacked at the foot of the plunging spar just above the pin rain. But they had hardly struck a blow in the shrieking wind before a sea swept over the stern of the *Maid*. The others, Peter among them, sprang into the rigging, but the sea caught the two men with the axes and buried them. When the deck cleared, they were both gone.

Another of the crew now seized an axe and wrapped a

lifeline about his waist. This was made fast to a ring in the deck and he set to with his axe on the mast. But his efforts were too late. The huge spar swung in a wild half circle, checked itself, and then, with a splintering crash, flung backward, snapping the forestays as though they were threads. The foremast plunged into the mainmast rigging, tearing through the heavy ropes as if they were cobwebs, then another huge sea drove aboard.

Peter caught a glimpse of the fallen mast rising from the sea as the dead are supposed to rise from their graves on Judgment Day. Then the lower end, which had ripped itself clear of the deck, leaving a huge hole over the forecastle, was flung like a battering ram against the inboard side of the ship's bow.

The *Maid of Malden* put her bow down in the water and never rose again.

Peter found himself lifted up on the crest of a wave and saw below him a welter of spars and rigging and a glimpse of the poop of the brig. He screamed and grabbed out blindly. Suddenly he was dropped down the back of the wave and caught in a tangle of ropes. He struggled for his breath in the roaring sea and the roaring wind, felt something solid under his arm and clung to it.

Another sea rose and rolled over them. Then another and another and another.

After a hurricane it was the custom of the people on the wilder parts of the South Carolina coast to leave whatever might be their normal work—the ploughing of their small plots or the sowing and reaping of crops, dependent upon the season—and comb the beaches for the aftermath of the storm.

The harvests they gleaned were well worth the time spent in this work, though the peoples of more settled communities would hardly think so. To a man who can walk into a shop and buy a pound of nails for a few pence, the finding of four or five nails in a piece of wood is hardly worth the trouble of their extraction. But to many of the people of South Carolina, in the latter half of the eighteenth century, a nail was a treasure used again and again, and half a dozen nails something that a man handed on to his son.

Those who combed the beaches were not, all of them, the coastal dwellers. Others came from the backwood mountains, thinking the journey of three or four days along animal paths and over the ridges of the mountains well recompensed if they came by a piece of brass or copper from a wrecked ship or a barrel of salted beef or, better still, a barrel of flour. The flour would, of course, be wet and useless in the outer parts. But the soggy dough thus formed provided a protection for the flour in the center which was useable and highly prized.

These dwellers in the interior, the great part of them Scotsmen driven out of their homeland after the rebellion of 1745, arrived in their search for storm treasure four or five days after the coastal dwellers. They had then to be content with whatever was left. Sometimes they bargained with the earlier arrivals for iron bolts, or pieces of iron or lead. Lead they especially sought. Their lives depended upon lead for out of it they made bullets.

The Maclaren of Spey was one such searcher from the interior of South Carolina. He had been the head of a clan numbering a hundred and twenty men, women and children when the Pretender landed in Scotland and raised the standard of revolt.

At Culloden Field the Pretender was defeated and the men of the clan killed—all but the Maclaren himself. He, with a price on his head and a gibbet waiting for him in Edinburgh, had fled to the American colonies and then to the highlands of the Carolinas.

This was the man then who, five days after the hurricane which destroyed the *Maid of Malden*, combed a wild section of the South Carolina coast. He was a singular figure—bearded and dressed in deerskin with, across his shoulders, a scrap of wool woven in the tartan of his clan. It was the sole remnant of a wardrobe which he had brought to the colonies twenty-five years previously. It was a last link with a piece of wind-blasted moorland between two granite mountain ranges in Scotland which was the home of the Maclaren of Spey.

It was late afternoon and there was not much to be found upon the beach. The Maclaren had gleaned only two or three nails and a brass hinge but he was a dogged man, not easily discouraged, and knew that often the heavier wreckage came ashore sometime after a hurricane, so that a search was still worthwhile.

He climbed to the top of a sand dune for a better view of the beach and saw, lying on the far side of the dune, a big section of a mast and some cordage and went toward this. He had passed this spot that morning and there had been nothing there, so he knew that the spar had only come in with the afternoon tide. When he got to the spar, his eyes quickened for there was a band of lead about it, to prevent the yard, seated at that point, from wearing into the mast. Then he saw over a small rise, a little way beyond, the figure of a boy.

The Maclaren went over to the boy and quickly searched

his pockets. He found a piece of beeswax, a horn button and a piece of rancid fat pork. He moved the boy over on his back and looked at him out of hard, fierce eyes. He was not moved by pity or tenderness. He had seen many dead children—some of them not merely dead but butchered. Two were his own sons slain at Culloden. Dead children were a commonplace in the Scottish Highlands after the defeat of the Pretender at Culloden. Cumberland the Butcher, uncle of the King of England, had been responsible for that.

The Maclaren was weighing the pros and cons of a problem. It was an important problem for him and it concerned this boy.

The problem was: Was the boy worth keeping alive? Or should he just leave him there and get on with what might be the more important task of taking the lead collar off the broken spar? It would take quite a while to do this and there was only an hour or two of daylight left.

The Maclaren squatted on his heels in the sand and thought about the lead and the boy, weighing which was the most valuable.

Chapter 11

MR. TREASER, foreman of the firm of Fielding & Co., Coopers, of Boston, shambled up the Strand in London, from Ludgate Circus toward Temple Bar, bewildered, uncomfortable, and conscious that he did not fit in this big city at all. He had indeed never been out of Boston before in his life. That his first journey abroad should have been the tremendous one of crossing the Atlantic to the capital of the British Empire left him utterly bewildered.

When Mr. Fielding had asked him to undertake the journey, he had adamantly refused to do so.

"I was born in Boston, Mr. Fielding, sir," he had said, "and I will die in Boston. And I do not care to see any other part of the world but Boston." But then Mr. Fielding had explained the reason why he must undertake the journey, and why no message might be sent by the mails, because of the uncertainty of the mails. And why the particular message which must be sent to Mr. John Treegate, and that at once, must be personally delivered to him, and not callously put into his hands by a complete stranger. And under the stress of these reasons and arguments, Mr. Treaser had agreed to cross the Atlantic, going from Boston to London.

Walking up the Strand now, he was still surprised that he had agreed and still in doubt as to whether all this was not all some kind of an hallucination from whose deceits he would soon emerge to face reality.

Because of the nature of his mission, Mr. Treaser had taken with him a particular suit, and this he now wore on his first day in London since debarking from the ship. It was a black suit with a long frock coat, or it had been black forty years before when he had received it from the hands of his father, now long dead.

At present it had that curious tinge of green which, like a mold on cheese, appears on black garments in their declining years. It was just such a suit to attract the attention of the London urchins and idlers of whom there were far more to be found in the Strand, Mr. Treaser was prepared to warrant, than in all the streets of his home city.

"Pipe the cockroach," one of them shouted from the doorway of a candlemaker's shop as Mr. Treaser shuffled past. The sally evoked considerable interest and efforts at besting it.

"What cellar did yer crawl out of, mister?" cried another. "Polly Broom's?" The sally of laughter which followed this remark convinced Mr. Treaser that Polly Broom, whoever she might be, was not the kind of woman with whom he would ever associate.

"Ain't a cockroach at all," cried a third. " 'E's a Cornish parson come to see if Queen Anne be dead." This jibe went home, for the very suit Mr. Treaser wore had been ordered by his father on the occasion of the death of Queen Anne. That was something over sixty years before.

Mr. Treaser felt that his present mission was one calling

for deep mourning and he was not conscious that the cut of the suit with its full frock coat reaching down below the knees was lamentably out of style. Indeed Mr. Treaser was conscious of very little in the world, as has been remarked before, but wood.

In the pocket of Mr. Treaser's long frock coat was a letter, and he stopped by Temple Bar, to which he had been directed as being close to the place he sought, to examine the address on the letter again. To do this it was necessary for him to put on his glasses, very small octagons of glass in black wire frames which had the property of magnifying anything held before them, though rendering Mr. Treaser almost completely blind for a few seconds after using them.

Ignoring the ruffians about him, Mr. Treaser first examined Temple Bar to be sure that it was indeed Temple Bar. "You'll find the head of Tolly the Forger above the bar on a pike," his informant had told him.

Mr. Treaser glanced up and saw that there was indeed a pike on top of the arch of the bar and on it a human head. He shuddered, for such things would never have been permitted in Boston, even in the most savage times. He concluded, and not for the first time that day, that Boston was an infinitely superior place to London.

Mr. Treaser put his glasses on his thin nose and, holding the letter up to them, read:

"John Treegate, Esq.,
218 Puddinghouse Lane,
Off the Strand. London."

He then gave the letter an over-all examination, paying close attention to the seals, for his crossing had been rough and a great deal of water had got into his chest in the hold where his letter had been placed. It was a letter dressed in as strange a manner as the bearer. The envelope, a sheet of parchment folded into a package, was decorated at each corner with a skull and crossbones. The edges of this envelope were trimmed with a wide border of black. And at the bottom of the letter was a drawing of a coffin, underneath which were the words "We shall rise from the dust."

Mr. Treaser examined the coffin and the words below carefully and shook his head. Then, first putting the letter and the glasses carefully away in his pocket, he took a firm grasp of his stick, eyed the grinning faces around him and snapped with surprising authority, "Out of my way, all of you." The command could not have been better delivered if it had come from a belted earl. The elderly foreman had brought up three generations of apprentices at least and was in no fear of mere youth and brawn.

He followed up his words with an upward swing of his stick which he brought down efficiently on the shin of one of his tormenters. This fellow let out a cry of surprise and pain and Mr. Treaser, showing a skill and strength remarkable in his years, followed up the blow with a crack at another fellow. In a moment all had fled, leaving him to continue his shuffle up the Strand undisturbed. Puddinghouse Lane, he had been told, was the second alley on the right after passing Temple Bar.

The alley proved to be surprisingly clean and neat compared with the litter and filth of the Strand. It was barred from the public by a chain stretched across the end of it, the chain itself being supervised by a stout man in livery of some sort. This individual wore a cocked hat with gold trimming around the brim and Mr. Treaser showed him his letter, asking to be admitted and directed to number two hundred and eighteen.

"Green door on your right, sir, about two hundred yards up," said the guard. "Boardinghouse it is for American gentlemen."

The elderly foreman nodded and shuffled up the Lane to the green door over which in nicely cut brass was the number "218."

A pleasant woman in a starched white cap and voluminous grey dress answered the door but gave the news that, although Mr. Treegate lived at that address, he was out at the present time.

"You may wait for him in his rooms and if you wish I will serve you a cup of tea in his parlor," she said.

"Oh dear," said Mr. Treaser. "Would you have any idea where he might be found?"

"At the Minister's, no doubt."

"The Minister?" asked Mr. Treaser.

"That would be Lord North's chambers off Whitehall. Mr. Treegate usually spends his days there with the other gentlemen from America. In the waiting room. They're all waiting to see the minister. Mr. Treegate has been waiting three months now."

"Three months?" echoed Mr. Treaser, aghast at the thought of so much time spent in idleness.

" 'Tis the way of politics, sir," said the woman. "If he misses but a day then it will be said that that was the very day when His Lordship was prepared to receive him. Thus he must be there at all times and thus His Lordship has attending him a great many people, each of them anxious to please him. It is said that some have waited so long upon His Lordship they have brought into His Lordship's waiting room their own chairs and tables and coffee services and servants so as to be the more comfortable.

"But here I stand chatting, sir, and you no doubt anxious for a dish of tea after your long voyage from America."

Mr. Treaser was surprised that Londoners knew instantly, by some miraculous process, that he was from the colonies. He was not conscious that his accent, with its flattened *a*, gave him away, and that even had he not uttered a word, there were certain mannerisms of the colonists, ways of standing and looking and walking, which betrayed his origin.

The Londoners—those of the better class—aped the manners of the court or what they took to be the manners of the court. They stood in a posture, with one leg forward the better to display the calf. Or they talked and at the same time made little flutters of their fingers, little swallows' swoops of their hands, which were thought to give grace to conversation. And all these were missing from the bearing of Mr. Treaser, who stood firmly upon his ancient feet and kept his hands in his pockets.

"Thank you, ma'am," he said. "But I do not think I will take the tea. I must see Mr. Treegate." His practical New England mind would not permit him, having come nearly three thousand miles, to drink a dish of tea at the end of it instead of getting on immediately with the object of his journey.

"It's a long way to Whitehall," said the good woman. "Whitehall lies in the city of Westminster, the better part of a mile from here. May I be so bold as to suggest that you take a chair to His Lordship?"

Mr. Treaser had never traveled in a sedan chair, a foreign contraption which the Duke of Marlborough was credited with introducing into England in Queen Anne's time, following his campaigns on the Continent. He did not particularly like the idea of being carried around by two of his fellow men.

On the other hand, a mile was a mile, so he swallowed his scruples and allowed the guard at the end of the lane to call a chair for him.

This was carried by two of the most evil-looking rascals Mr. Treaser had ever clapped eyes upon. They looked him over as he got in and exchanged a broad wink with each other, the meaning of which was lost for the moment on Mr. Treaser. He discovered its significance half an hour later when the chairmen, having taken him up a noisome alley, in a very foul part of the city, put him down and said they would take him no further unless he paid them each a shilling there and then.

There was nothing to do but to pay them the shilling, whereupon the two of them disappeared into a squalid tavern and drank each of them a measure of gin. In the meantime a horde of urchins collected around the sedan chair and, having peered inside and made some very uncomplimentary remarks about the occupant, decided it would be the best of sport to tip the chair over in the filthy street. They set about doing this when the chairmen returned and a free-for-all took place between the chairmen and the mob before Mr. Treaser was finally rescued and taken on his way.

He had further difficulties on arrival at Lord North's chambers, where he had to part with two more shillings to the chairmen. For it seemed that it was a great privilege indeed, extended only to select people, to be allowed to as much as wait upon His Lordship. Before the gate there were two liveried servants whose duty it was to keep the world away from His Lordship. These refused to let Mr. Treaser pass inside, though they agreed that they would take his letter in for him.

The old foreman, however, would not be parted from the letter, and finally gained admittance by abandoning his scruples against bribery and giving each of them a shilling.

He was then allowed inside but had to go through the same process with an underfootman, an overfootman, a gentleman who seemed to be Guardian of the Stairs and another gentleman who was Guardian of the Door. All in all, it cost Mr. Treaser a ruinous seven shillings to as much as gain admittance to His Lordship's waiting room.

This proved to be an enormous chamber, bigger than the elderly foreman had ever seen. It was crowded with gentlemen dressed in the height of fashion. Some had coats of pale blue silk and others ones of scarlet taffeta. Some had breeches of white satin and others breeches of red velvet. All had waist-coats elaborated with needlework in flower patterns or hung with festoons of lace. And the lace of the waistcoats found a counterpart in little gushes or spurts of lace from the sleeves of their coats, from the tops of their pockets and around their throats. The effect was as exotic as a glimpse of so many birds of paradise in a cage.

When Mr. Treaser entered, these various sublime gentlemen were busying themselves doing nothing. Some stood by windows, peering down in the streets below; some sprawled in chairs with an elegant leg over the elegant arm of the chair and affected sleep. Others stood and quizzed their fellows through gold-edged quizzing glasses and one amused himself by blowing bubbles through a long clay pipe.

All these then, on the entry of Mr. Treaser, interrupted

their idleness to turn slowly and deliberately and look at him. Those with quizzing glasses quizzed him from head to foot. The man with the clay pipe, who had been blowing bubbles, dropped his pipe upon the floor, breaking it in an elaborate affectation of astonishment. Men who had been staring out of windows or at pictures upon the walls moved slowly to examine the slight, grey-haired figure in the black coat, green with age, who had invaded their premises.

"Stap me, Harvey," said one eventually, "I cannot believe it. Here's the oddest fish ever to swim into His Lordship's pool. Pipe the coat, I beg you. Oh, I shall die, sir. I shall die." Having said this, this individual looked around most carefully for a chair and collapsed most gracefully into it.

But at this point Mr. Treaser decided he had had as much as he could stand of London. The city had put upon him most grievously ever since he had set foot in it and he was prepared now to accept no more. He was not a man of the mildest of dispositions and there was a hard core of Boston pride buried behind his unprepossessing physical appearance. He therefore advanced into the room until he came to the popinjay who had collapsed so elegantly into the chair, and poked him vigorously in his flowered waistcoat with the end of his stick.

"You, sir," snapped Mr. Treaser in his flat Boston voice. "Where can I find Mr. John Treegate?" The elegant gentleman came out of his swoon and opened his pale blue eyes in genuine astonishment. No one except his personal servant had ever dared to as much as lay a hand upon his waistcoat and here was this ancient and angry man spotting it with the end of his dirty stick.

"Harvey," he bleated. "Harvey . . ." And he swooned again, this time without pretense.

Mr. Treaser turned, looking around at the others who had dropped their quizzing glasses in astonishment and were gaping at him.

"Do any of you popinjays know where I can find Mr. John Treegate of Boston?" he asked.

"Oh God," said one. "Boston. He's one of those colonials." Then someone cried, "Mr. Treaser, whatever brings you to London?" and John Treegate came forward and took the old foreman by the hand and gave it such a wringing that he grimaced. He then led the old foreman away to a corner of the room.

"Old friend," cried Mr. Treegate, "I cannot tell you how glad I am to see you. And in London of all places. But what brings you here? Come. I am all impatience. It is not the Boston Massacre, is it? We have had all the news of that, and it has horribly damaged our cause with His Lordship."

"No," said Mr. Treaser, easing himself into a chair, "it is not the massacre." And now that he had come to the culminating point of his mission, he did not know how to begin. He did not know whether to produce the letter in his pocket and hand it to the delighted man before him, or whether to attempt to soften the blow first with a few introductory phrases.

But if there were such introductory phrases, Mr. Treaser could not lay tongue to them. He reached in his pocket and took out the letter.

"It's for you, Mr. Treegate," he said. And he added with a great depth of feeling, "I am very sorry."

John Treegate took the letter and when he saw all the marks of death upon it—the skull and crossbones, the deep black edging of the envelope and the coffin with below it the words "We shall rise from the dust"—his face blanched.

"Is it Peter?" he asked.

He tore open the letter and read the contents and the foreman, watching him, saw John Treegate age twenty years, as it were, in two minutes. The letter was from Mr. Fielding and read:

"My dear friend:

"There is no way in which I can tell you without great suffering to yourself of the tragedy which has befallen your son, Peter, whom you left in my charge but six short months ago. I can only state bluntly that the boy has disappeared and I can only add that he is believed dead.

"The circumstances I will put forth plainly and, I trust, with as little hurt as possible to you. The boy had accompanied me to the house of Mr. Sam Adams with the purpose that he should light me home should I be long delayed there. However, our business taking a greater time than I had expected, and the weather being severe, I thought it better to send him home with the lantern by himself. The time was not late, being only nine o'clock in the evening. Believe me, my friend, I did this with the very best of intentions and with no thought that any harm could befall the boy, I have not ceased to upbraid myself for letting him go from that moment to this.

"That was the last I or anyone else saw of him. He never reached my home. He was seen by none of his friends. The city watch know nothing of his disappearance. He vanished.

"I cannot elaborate upon this nor think of any motive for his disappearance nor why anyone should set upon him in the streets. He carried no money upon him and my first thought was that he had found the life of an apprentice too harsh. I know that he met with the usual amount of rough

treatment at the hands of his fellows. But it was no more, I assure you, than other boys have faced, and he seemed to bear up under it in a manly way. His fellow apprentice, Golding, with whom he had been a close friend, assures me that Peter was all in all happy, though he missed you and I understand that he was much cast down at the prospect of your London visit lasting longer than you had expected.

"When I heard of this from Golding, it occurred to me that the boy, in his loneliness, might have got himself aboard a ship, hoping to go to you in England. I had, of course, given him your address. I was grasping for any clue, however wild, which might lead to a discovery of his whereabouts. I made inquiries concerning all ships which left Boston that night or any time the following two days. But only one vessel left the city and I think it better that Mr. Treaser should tell you of it as it would be most dangerous to commit any mention of this vessel to writing.

"It was not, however, bound for England, and news has now arrived in Boston that it was lost in a hurricane.

"I have done all I may—indeed I continue doing all I may—to get any news of the boy. I have posted a reward on my own surety of five hundred pounds for any news of his whereabouts, but nothing has been forthcoming. I have in short done all that you yourself could have done; but without result.

"One circumstance leads me to believe, painful as it is to say this, that the boy is dead. The night that he disappeared, the body of Mr. James Wheeler, whom you will remember as one of the more prosperous merchants of this city, was found dying upon the Long Wharf. He had been stabbed several times in the back and robbed. The knife with which this foul murder had been committed was found lying near the

corpse and was identified as a knife which had been given to your son Peter.

"It seems more than probable that the boy, on his way to my house, had met Mr. Wheeler and had been persuaded to light the gentleman to his house on the Long Wharf. The two were set upon and Peter drew his knife to defend himself. There seems little doubt that he was overcome, killed and his body thrown into the river. The savages who were guilty of this foul deed were unable or unwilling to dispose of Mr. Wheeler's body in the same way, and left the boy's knife beside it, perhaps with the thought that he might be blamed for the murder.

"My friend, believe me, I suffer heavily in having to relay to you this terrible news. I have blamed myself continually and can find no crumb of comfort to offer you. The disappearance—nay, be brave, my friend, the death of your boy—will be a charge against me until I myself am claimed by the grave.

"Your friend and sharer in this cup of sorrow,

Thomas Fielding."

When Mr. Treegate had read this letter, he let it drop to the floor and bowed his head and, though his eyes were squeezed shut, still the tears were wrung from them and fell down his face. He was a brave man and a stout one, but the impact of this overwhelming grief was too much for him.

Mr. Treaser, to whom long decades of life had brought many years of suffering, rose and put his hands on his shoulders, yearning, in his tired, crotchety old heart, to give comfort by this awkward but simple gesture.

Then, recalling where they were, he turned a fierce look upon the splendidly dressed gentlemen about, and raised the other man up.

"We had better leave," he said.

The two walked across the room and out of the door and the splendid gentlemen in His Lordship's waiting room looked nervously at each other.

Nothing had been replaced by something. They had seen a man whom they knew to be brave and stubborn in tears and the sight made them uncomfortable.

They reached for their snuff boxes and fingered their quizzing glasses and tried to forget it.

Chapter 12

PETER TREEGATE, washed ashore on the deserted South Carolina beach, owed his life to the decision of the Maclaren of Spey that it was just possible the boy might be valuable. In precisely what way the boy might prove valuable, the Maclaren was not at all sure. At the back of his mind there was a faint hope that he might belong to someone somewhere, and this someone might be willing to pay a reward for his return—should it ever be possible to find this person. But more likely, the Scotsman argued, the boy was an orphan. In that case his value would depend entirely on his ability to become a personal servant to the Scottish chieftain, bereft of a clan by the terrible massacre of Culloden and his own subsequent flight to the American colonies.

The Scotsman was in no hurry to save the boy. Arriving at the decision that he might be worth saving, he satisfied himself that he was breathing, though but faintly, and then turned to the work of getting the collar of lead off the broken spar. There was real value here. Five pounds of lead could be converted into forty or fifty bullets. And forty or fifty bullets in the Carolina backwoods was a treasure indeed.

The lead salvaged, the Maclaren tied it with a piece of cord around his waist and turned to Peter again. He raised him to a sitting position, supporting him against his knee, and fumbled in a pouch slung at his waist for a small metal flask. This he unstoppered, pouring into Peter's mouth a drop or two of white liquid. Then he looked anxiously into the boy's face to watch the effect that this remedy might have.

Its effect was slight, but satisfactory. Peter's eyes fluttered open for a second and then shut again. The Maclaren put him down, glanced around, perhaps to see if any more wreckage was being washed ashore while he was engaged in this task of rescue, and proceeded to rub the boy's hands briskly and roughly between his own. He put a great deal of vigor into this, jerking Peter's shoulders and arms with the effort; the boy again opened his eyes, perhaps in protest, and his lips formed a word, though no sound came from them. No sound was necessary. The Scotsman knew that the boy, who had patently been in the water many days, was weak as much from thirst as from exposure to the sea and the merciless washing of the waves.

He gave him a drink of water, again from a flask hung from his waist. He forced the water into Peter's mouth and the deliciously cool and sweet liquid gave the boy a swift measure of strength.

He moved his head aside, opened his eyes and looked at the Scotsman.

The Maclaren grunted. "Ye'll live," he said. He spoke neither with relief nor with satisfaction. He was merely making a statement based upon his knowledge of how much suffering a human being can be exposed to without dying.

He gave Peter another sip of water and then lifted him up, putting him across his shoulder like a sack. The Maclaren was a small man, very small; he hardly topped five feet four inches. But he lifted the boy with ease and walked with him across the loose sand into the palmetto scrub. There he paused to collect a long rifle, beautifully chased and ornamented about the butt with silver insets. It was the rifle of the Maclaren chiefs—a weapon upward of a hundred years old.

He had used it at Culloden on the Redcoats and he now used it in the backwoods on the Indians. He slung the rifle over his free shoulder by a bandolier and went on walking.

In all, he walked with the boy a hundred miles over mountains and down valleys, and up granite-strewn slopes and through stinking swamps covered with vicious sawgrass.

It was no great feat for the Maclaren. He had walked twenty miles a day with a full-grown sheep over his shoulders many a time, often in a blizzard. It was just possible that the boy he carried might be as valuable as a sheep and for this reason, and this alone, he carried him.

In all that journey, which took six days, Peter never recovered sufficient strength to do more than stand and that only shakily. His muscles had become atrophied from exposure and even when he stood up, at the rough insistence of the Maclaren, he would in a minute be overwhelmed by a blackness and fall to the ground, sweating violently and trembling. Indeed it was an additional two weeks, after they had reached the highlander's mountain shack, before the boy regained the use of his legs to any extent.

This shack lay on the slope of a mountain, which formed but one of a chain running roughly from northeast to southwest. A thousand feet below was a thickly forested valley. The trees of the forest were mostly conifers, pines, firs and occasionally spruce. But there were to be found also an occasional beech and ash and elm which gave a nice touch of variety to the forests.

The boy had never known a forest so thick. The trunks of the trees rose like pillars from the floor, which was covered with a thick growth of underbrush. At times these trees were so close together that it was impossible to pass between them. Even the game paths skirted these thick clumps where some special richness of the soil had produced such a profusion.

In the forests there were always sounds, day or night. At first these sounds seemed to Peter to be lonely, to be full of a great mournfulness which emphasized how desolate the area was of human life. The wind soughing in the trees, the cries of the birds, the chatter of chipmunks and squirrels and occasionally the howl of wolves filled the boy with fear as he lay, for two weeks, gradually regaining his strength in the Scotsman's shack.

It was as strange a dwelling as might be imagined. Originally it had been nothing but a shelter constructed by leaning some felled trees against a boulder which thrust out of the face of the mountain for twelve or more feet. The boulder formed one wall, the trees the other, but they were wall and roof as well for they met eight or nine feet overhead, in the apex of a triangle the base of which was the floor.

The earth of the floor, however, the Scotsman had scooped out to provide himself with a cellar, now covered over with rough-hewn planks. He had improved further upon his dwelling by adding another room, all of logs, which stood atop the boulder whose upper surface was about eight feet square. This room was in reality a separate house, for it could not be reached from the original dwelling. It had to be entered from outside by climbing up a ladder.

The Maclaren's cooking and eating arrangements were of the most primitive sort. He cooked upon a stone outside the lower shack, making a fire of pine knots and roasting his meat on this over a spit. When he wished to bake bread, he made the dough out of crushed corn—it bore little similarity to flour—and put this in the hot ashes of the fire. It would be burned black as charcoal on the outside. But the inside was soft and edible and seemingly nutritious, for on this diet of roasted meat and rough cornbread, Peter's strength slowly returned to him, until the day came when he was able to stagger uncertainly out of the hut and look around him.

His memory, to the Scotsman's disgust, had become as atrophied as his leg muscles. For some time he could not even recall his own name. The Maclaren told him that he had found him on the shore and therefore he must be a cabin boy of a ship. But for some time this seemed to Peter a most surprising circumstance. He did not know who he was or what he had done previously in his life, but when he thought about being at sea, this did not seem to him to have been his mode of living at all.

Part of his memory returned one day when he was trying to make a fire with some green pine wood. It seemed that he had gone through this process several times before. And then he remembered the galley on the brig and the name Hoyle came tumbling into his mind and with it his own name.

"Peter," he shouted suddenly. "My name's Peter. Peter...." But he could not remember his surname. He tried hard and remembered Gabby and Captain Pleashed. But he could not recall how he had come to be on this ship nor even what was the name of the ship. He made the greatest effort of which he was capable. But there seemed to be something dark and terrible connected with his being at sea and his mind refused to contemplate whatever this was.

Eventually Peter gave it up. He knew that he was Peter and that he had been shipwrecked and found by the Maclaren. If more came to him it would have to be without effort, for his mind recoiled from effort.

The fact that he could remember only part of his name and little of his previous life had the most singular effect upon the Maclaren. At first he was angry for the boy could not be restored to his master or his parents and a reward received which might amount to perhaps as much as ten shillings.

Then he decided that the boy was bewitched, for the Maclaren was full of dark Celtic superstitions which had a stronger grip upon him than Christianity, which had been the faith of his people for a mere thousand years. They had been pagans much longer. Indeed the Maclaren mixed Christianity up with the old pagan beliefs of his forebears and, when he had killed a deer or other animal, would make a small cut with his hunting knife in some part of himself.

Peter asked him the reason for this one day, when he felt he knew the strange, savage Scotsman better.

"Ye cann' spill anither's bluid wi' oot spilling some of yer ane," said the Maclaren, scowling. "Itherways, the curse o' the dead is on ye."

Holding then that Peter was bewitched, the highlander constantly asked his opinion about such matters as whether it was a good day to cut wood or a good day to go hunting or whether there would be any harm, at a particular time, in gathering some of the berries which grew in profusion in the woods. Nonetheless he used Peter with great harshness when the boy had recovered his strength, and beat him unmercifully if the fire were out or, though lighted, not glowing sufficiently for his satisfaction. He would go into sudden and appalling bursts of fury and seemingly without cause and throw the boy out of the rude shelter and tell him be gone and never return. And then, an hour or so later, he would go through the woods calling to him and pleading with him to come back.

Once he beat Peter so badly that the boy was black and blue for several days, his eyes swollen so that he could hardly open them. But when he thought about it later, Peter had to admit that he probably deserved the beating.

The occasion arose when the two had gone together through the woods to bring back the hindquarters of a deer that the Maclaren had killed on the previous day. He had packed both the forequarters himself as well as the head but had left the remainder for the next day, because it had grown dark.

The remains of the carcass had been cached by the highlander on the fork of a beach which lay a quarter of a mile down the valley. Their way lay down several slopes of scree, or loose stones, and past a number of big boulders jutting out the side of the mountain.

The Maclaren went ahead and was in a surly mood for he held it against Peter that the boy was not strong enough, though his personal servant, to bring the quarters back himself. This surliness lessened the Scotsman's usual sense of awareness and, when they got in among the boulders, a bear came trundling along the game path with two cubs behind her.

Peter was carrying the Scotsman's gun and was paralyzed

by the sudden appearance of the animal. It was the first
bear he had ever seen and looked, at such close quarters,
monstrous. The bear gave a roar of warning to her cubs and
rose on her massive hindlegs.

"The gun," shouted the Maclaren. But Peter was frozen
with fright. He could not have moved a muscle and with
a scream of rage the bear charged on the little highlander.
What happened next Peter did not see. He shut his eyes
and crouched against the boulder, the gun falling useless at
his feet. He remained like this, hearing the roaring of the
bear and the scattering of stones and the cries of the Scotsman for his gun.

And then he was jerked to his feet and found the Maclaren before him. The Scotsman's face was a mass of blood
and his eyes were the eyes of a demon. He beat the boy
about the face, blow upon blow, threw him to the ground
and picked him up and beat him again. He left off only
when rocking with fatigue. And then he stood over the
frightened, slobbering boy and said, "Ye bluidy Sassanach
(Saxon) whelp. Would ye let me be killed while ye ha' me
gun? Better die wi' yer friend than live and ha' him dead.
Remember that."

Peter did remember. The savagery of the beating, and
his own remorse at his cowardice and panic, the thought
that the bear might readily have killed the Maclaren who
had saved his life—these things combined grew into a hard
determination that he would never again shrink from any
conflict, whatever the odds. The determination did not come
suddenly. It was the growth of some weeks. And, in no small
measure, it was the work of the Maclaren himself.

The Scotsman brooded over the incident for several days.
He had been clawed across the face by the bear, which he had

killed finally with his hunting knife. It occurred to him that the boy did not know how to use a gun and, furthermore, did not know how to fight.

This latter was extremely hard for the Maclaren to believe, for he could not remember a time in his life when he had not known how to fight. He could fight with his hands and his feet, with a gun or a knife or a cudgel or a pike or any kind of weapon. It was an instinct with him, an instinct and a training, for among the members of his clan, quarrels had been settled not by words but by blows with knives and swords and often death and wounding.

But it was just possible that this boy had no knowledge of fighting and so he determined to teach him, not out of interest in the boy, but to provide a measure of safety for himself.

He started first with the rifle. He explained its working parts carefully and patiently. He explained how the weight of the bullet used had to be balanced by the amount of powder used. He explained how to shape a flint for the hammer and how to prime the pan and how too much powder and too tight a bullet might bring a backflash that would blind the user or, worse, explode the breeching. He explained about judging the wind, and how at dusk and dawn, when the air was cold, objects a quarter of a mile off seemed to be just a few yards away, being magnified by the very density of the air.

All this and a hundred other circumstances bearing on the use of the rifle he went into in elaborate detail. Then he took a horn of powder and selected some pebbles; using these as bullets and very little powder, he gave Peter lessons in marksmanship. The boy proved to have a talent for guns and brought down a wild goat as his first kill. The Maclaren grunted his approval.

Side by side with the lessons in the use of the rifle came others in taking and giving punishment—in fighting.

The Scotsman was far from gentle here. When he struck Peter, he did so with force and sent him flying. But the boy would get up again and come in for more, sometimes whimpering with pain and nerves. Yet he came on and soon he learned to keep a cool head, dodge the blows and not pay any attention to punishment suffered. Several times, brought to his knees, he felt he could not rise again to face more punishment. But up he got and then the Maclaren would stop.

"Ye're no a man yet," he would say. "When ye're a man, I'll beat ye whenever ye get to yer feet until there's no fight left in ye. But yer a boy now and that would break yer spirit. A man's spirit is never broken."

Peter thought many times that the day would never come when he was not aching with bruises. But his body toughened and he even came to look forward to his bouts at wrestling or fisticuffs with the Maclaren.

The experience worked a deep change in him. It brought him something which he had never had before and which, up to that moment, he was not aware he lacked. And that was independence based upon a respect for his own abilities. He was no longer fearful of the soughing of the trees and the noises of the forests. At nighttime he heard the hunting cries of the wolves and the crashing of a desperate stag through the underbrush and his flesh no longer crawled with fear. Now he listened to the notes of the wolves and learned to tell whether there were two or three or a pack of a dozen. He learned to judge their distance from him. In short, he learned to put aside fear and calmly to weigh the dangers which surrounded him.

With this came an immense peace. He merged into the primitive life of the forest and found it not always menacing, though there was always the need for awareness.

Once, in the hot summer, out alone in the wilds, he jumped from a bank down onto a rock and saw at his feet a big rattlesnake, as surprised as he was and in that moment coiling to strike.

A few months previously he would have been frozen like a rabbit and would have died of the venom. Now he leaped up hard and fierce, pinning the writhing body of the snake under his feet when he came down. He held the reptile with one foot and stamped on it with the other and jumped clear. The snake slithered off the rock with its spine broken and Peter did not even bother to look further for it. He was not glad that he had killed the snake. He took no joy in the act. He had done what was necessary to defend himself and he had done it quickly and competently and from this and this alone he drew satisfaction.

Peter Treegate, one time Boston apprentice, who had fled in panic from a dead man and his own wild fears, was not a child any longer.

He was a boy developing to manhood.

Chapter 13

FOR THE FIRST several months of his stay with the half savage Scotsman, Peter saw no other human being. He wondered during his first weeks in the primitive shack whether there were no Indians in the forests and was in an agony of fear whenever the Maclaren of Spey set off on a hunting expedition and remained away overnight—sometimes for two nights. But when he questioned the highlander, he was told that the nearest tribe was twenty miles away and that they had learned not to come into the territory of the Maclaren.

This was the first intimation Peter had that the Scotsman regarded the land about as his. He gradually came to realize that the Maclaren claimed the whole of the side of the mountain and the valley below him. He was in fact establishing in Carolina that claim to territory he had once had as the head of a clan in the Scottish highlands. He was as sovereign a lord in the Carolina mountains as he had ever been in the Scottish wilds. Peter noted many times a peeled stick which was hung over the entrance to the shack. He thought this was some sort of superstition of the man's but one day asked the Maclaren about it.

" Tis the tara," said the Maclaren.

"What's a tara?" Peter asked.

"The symbol o' the chief o' the clan," said the Maclaren with withering scorn. "It marks the chief's house." The Scotsman had also a beautiful broach of heavy silver, obviously extremely old. This pinned the rag of tartan to his deerskin jerkin and Peter discovered that this was the Tara broach, again worn only by the chieftain, the mark of his authority over the clan which he ruled.

The Maclaren, then, still thought of himself as a clan chieftain, a right which he held by descent. Normally extremely uncommunicative—it was not uncommon for him to say but half a dozen words in the course of the day—he would talk at length about his descent, reeling off a list of names to prove that he was the chieftain of the Maclarens.

Peter could not make much sense out of the Maclaren's family tree. But it seemed that the clan were kinsmen to half the clans of Scotland, though the kinship might depend on as narrow a thread as the marriage of someone's sixth cousin to someone else's half cousin, an event which had taken place two hundred years previously.

The Maclaren also explained the system of fosterage, common among the ancient Irish and the Scots who were, he said, a branch of the Irish peoples. Indeed, the Maclarens of Spey were kin to the MacClunes of Rathdhu in Ulster, the MacClunes of Rathdhu being the stock from which the Maclarens had sprung in their emigration from Ireland to Scotland.

Fosterage, the Maclaren explained, was essentially a method of preserving peace among the clansmen. The chieftain of a rival clan would exchange sons with his enemy. Each handed a son into the other's care and the boys were brought up from babyhood to manhood by their father's enemy. The boys thus exchanged were not hostages. They were pledges of good faith. And any chieftain who killed a boy sent to him in "fosterage" was himself killed by his own clansmen.

A year after Peter had been with the Maclaren, the highlander announced that he had decided to take the boy into fosterage.

"I canna' do it right," he said, "for yer faither should gie me a sword for ye and a targe (shield) and a porringer. And I dinna' ken who yer faither is. But I mind that the Black Buchanan took a lad intae fosterage that he found in the hills, and the clan accepted the wee lad and he died wi' the Black Buchanan at the Burn o' Bannock."

"The Burn of Bannock?" cried Peter. "Do you mean the Battle of Bannockburn? That was four hundred years ago."

The Maclaren reeled out a list of names, reviewing his ancestry to the time of the battle, and then said calmly, "Aye, it were aboot that. Aboot four hundred years ago. Angus o' the Shieling killed the Earl of Warpen in the first charge, and died of the Sassenach's curse a year later tae the day."

Having satisfied himself on this point, and concluded that what was done four hundred years previously by the Black Buchanan might be done by himself with equal propriety, he drew his hunting knife. He then took the boy's right arm and made a cut in it above the wrist; then, baring his own right arm, he did the same to himself.

"Put yer bluid on mine," he said and since Peter did not understand, he took the boy's wrist and pressed the cut he had made against his own wound.

"Your bluid and mine," he said solemnly, "mingle now and are one bluid. Yer my man and I yours and who hurts you hurts me. So it will be while we draw breath."

He then explained very seriously that there could never again be any question of separation or individuality between the two of them; that Peter, for instance, might not marry without the Maclaren's approving, and that the Maclaren's quarrel must now become Peter's quarrel. The boy was deeply impressed but dismayed at the thought of sharing the Maclaren's quarrels for, from what he heard of his history, the Maclarens of Spey, for all the intermingling bonds of fosterage and kinship, had a host of quarrels with every other clan in the Scottish highlands.

A little while after this ceremony, the Maclaren announced that they should visit Thomastown, for he was short of powder and supplies could be had there.

Peter had by now learned that there was a settlement by that name "a wee step beyond the mountain," as Maclaren put it. He was delighted at the prospect and eagerly packed the dressed deerskins which the Maclaren had prepared, and which he would trade in Thomastown for powder, lead and salt.

The journey took three days. It was not one mountain that had to be crossed but several ranges of mountains. They started in late September and the forests were dried out and strangely quiet, for there was not a breath of air stirring. The heat, even in the gloom of the conifer forests, was oppressive and the smell of resin in the still air almost overwhelming. But this heat was as nothing compared with that which rose in shimmering waves from the bared places on the mountain slopes which were covered with sheet upon sheet of white rocks. These places were too hot to be walked over, for the heat from the rocks seared their feet through their moccasins. They had to be skirted or negotiated at nighttime.

The Maclaren set a pace which was hard to match. He would rise before dawn, and they had eaten and were some miles on their way before the sun broke over the top of the mountains. Before setting out, the Maclaren would drink his fill of water; drink so much in fact that it seemed impossible that so small a man could hold such a quantity. But then he would drink nothing again until the next dawn, and he scowled when Peter, his mouth gluey with thirst, wished to stop at a trickle of water at midday to quench his thirst. It was worse than useless drinking in the heat, the Maclaren said, and dangerous too. The water chilled the stomach and brought cramps. A man should drink only once a day and that when it was cool. Then, however, he should drink a great quantity, whether he was thirsty or not.

Peter tried this and found that following the Maclaren's advice he did not suffer much from thirst during the day.

Gradually the mountains became less steep, their place being taken by rolling hills between which were vast acreages of swamp and sawgrass, with palmettos growing in clumps here and there.

These swamps, which gave off an unhealthy reek, were nonetheless filled with wildfowl. Ducks, geese, cranes and storks rose in clouds from them. In parts of these swamps wild rice was growing, and the Maclaren filled two skin bags with the grain, and cached them to be picked up on the return journey.

Thomastown lay by a muddy river at the edge of a thick forest of live oak and palmetto in one of these swampy valleys. The deer trail the two had been following gradually widened to become something which might be identified as a footpath and then as a road, though it was a road of black dust which rose in clouds up to their knees as they walked. When they got fairly onto this road, and with Thomastown "a wee step away," according to the Maclaren (he had no other measure of distance but "a wee step"), he stopped like an animal suspicious of danger, turned his head slowly around and sniffed the air.

"Do ye smell anything?" he asked.

Peter sniffed but found nothing strange to remark upon.

The Maclaren jerked his head as a signal to the boy to leave the rude road and they went into the live oak and palmetto by the side.

"What's the matter?" Peter asked.

"Carrion," said the Scotsman. He took his rifle, unwrapped the piece of deerskin which was bound around the lock to keep the pan dry, and primed the pan. The piece was already loaded, for even the Maclaren could not load the big rifle with powder and shot wrapped in a greased patch of deerskin in less than a minute.

The Scotsman, satisfied that the rifle was now ready to fire, moved on silently in the shadow of the live oaks and Peter followed him. When they had gone about a hundred yards, the highlander stopped and sniffed again. A big blue fly whirled out of the shadow and settled on his shoulder and was quickly joined by several more. The Scotsman looked at the flies and, all his caution leaving him, said, "We're too late."

He stepped out of the woods onto the road and set off briskly in the direction of the town, the boy following him, thoroughly mystified.

He did not remain mystified for long. Forty yards down the road they came across the body of a child—a girl of perhaps four years. She was dead and covered with flies. Beside her was a small doll made of rags and straw. They found more bodies further on and, rounding a bend, a mass of vultures rose on lazy wings into the air and settled down again upon the shambles of what had been the trading post and settlement of Thomastown.

The slaughter was appalling. Not a building stood except two walls of what had once been the combined fort and trading post of the settlement. The dead lay singly or in groups of two or three. Some had been shot, but most had been killed with cudgels or axes. The sight made Peter sick but it stirred a vague unrest in his mind. Somewhere, sometime, he had seen some such thing before—people violently killed and lying in their own blood on the ground. The blood had looked black, as it did now. But where and when? His mind recoiled from the problem and he put it aside.

They went grimly through the ruins of the little settlement looking for a sign of life, but found only the vultures and the clouds of swarming flies. The Maclaren's face was hard and his eyes burning with hate. The sight reminded him of another scene, the village of his clan after the Redcoats of Cumberland the Butcher had been there.

He went into the remnants of the fort, where the bodies were the thickest, and, ignoring the dead, looked now for what he could salvage that might be of use. He found several rifles but their stocks were broken and then, moving a body, found beneath it a blood-soaked gun which he gave silently to Peter. It seemed to be the only weapon which had survived the massacre whole. He searched for three hours before he found sufficient powder to satisfy him, and half a sack of salt. In all this time Peter followed him but the Scotsman said not a word.

Then, with the gun, now Peter's, and the powder and the salt, he walked out of the shambles of the settlement and, avoiding the road, plunged straight into the live-oak forests. He walked until dusk that day, headed for the mountains whose foothills were twenty miles away, and in all that time he never said a word. But when he had eaten his evening meal he said, "I maun call the mountain folk together for revenge."

He did not explain further and it was not necessary. The Maclaren was no kin to the slaughter victims. The Indians had not molested him in his shack. But his memories had been stirred and the blood spilled called for a bloody payment. King's men or Indians, Redcoats or Cherokees and Painted Sticks, they were all of them the enemies of his sort.

The two did not return to the Scotsman's dwelling in the mountains, but struck instead for the southeast where, after two days, they came upon three shacks in the bottom of a valley. These were also the homes of fugitives from the rebellion of Forty-Five. There were five men and three women in the shacks and when the Maclaren neared them, he cupped his hands and gave out a high scream that echoed from mountain top to mountain top. A huge bearded man came out of one of the shacks with a rifle in his hand and stood waiting for them.

"Thomastown is wiped oot," said the Maclaren. "There's not a wee bairn left alive."

The bearded man looked around the mountains which ringed the valley and said, "I'll send Tobbie and Davie north tae the McClintocks and Blakes. I'll gae east tae the Murphies O' Dondailey."

The Maclaren nodded. "I'll pass the word south to the Burtons and Shippens," he said. "I'll be back in three days."

He nodded to Peter. "Ye've no met him," he said. "He's a Sassenach but I'm fostering him."

The big man looked at Peter and said to Maclaren, "Ye ha' need o' a son. But ye should marry, mon, for ye're kinless and clanless these twenty years."

"There's time enough for marrying," said the Maclaren and without another word went on past the cabins, heading south, followed by Peter.

Three days later they were back; there had gathered at the three cabins some score of mountain men. They were all the wildest-looking men, dressed in skins and carrying rifles. Two, like the Maclaren, wore a piece of tartan on their shoulders but none carried the tara broach of a chieftain. For this reason perhaps, the Maclaren was their acknowledged leader.

There was little enough discussion of plans. They all knew the tribe which had perpetrated the massacre of Thomastown—knew it from its past reputation for bloody deeds in which some of them had lost members of their families. They talked of the Indians of the tribe as they would talk of a marauding pack of wolves. They were determined now to exterminate it and they moved off in groups of two or three for the valley where the tribe had its village.

This valley was an additional two days' journey away. It was a small place between the sides of heavily forested mountains. The forests were tinder dry and the mountain men had already decided, without mutual discussion, the weapon of extermination which would be used.

That weapon was to be fire.

When they had arrived near the Indian village, the Maclaren, and the big bearded man, who was known by no other name than Dirk, went forward to scout. The Maclaren took Peter with him.

They circled around one side of the mountains overlooking the village and slipped quietly down through the trees until they were on a precipice of rock from which they could peer down on the Indian settlement.

The others of the party meanwhile had ranged themselves on the other side of the village and lower down the valley in front of it. The tents of the village were arranged in a rough circle around a large central area which Peter guessed would be the common council ground of the tribe. In the middle of this central area were two stout poles, perhaps twenty feet apart, with a line strung between them.

On the line a number of tattered things hung limp in the sun. It was a few seconds before the boy realized that these were lengths of human hair, taken from the victims of the Thomastown massacre. There was another stout pole some distance off and a prisoner was hanging from this. Even at the distance Peter could tell he was dead. The air was very still and hot and the rock from which they peered burned the naked flesh when they touched it.

From looking at the village, Peter turned to the thick dry woods which surrounded it and saw a small trickle of smoke curling up through the trees. Then another trickle of smoke appeared behind the village, perhaps three hundred yards away and then another. In a matter of seconds there were half a dozen of them and then the smoke disappeared, to be replaced by white sheets of flame which roared upward in the quiet air with a sound curiously like the raging of the sea. Above this roar came a burst of sharp crackles, and pines first and larches were suddenly transformed into a mass of fire which ringed the village.

The Indians came tumbling out of their tents like bees from so many hives. There was but one route of escape for them—the area at the lower end of the valley which the mountain men had not fired. They streamed for it and suddenly that end of the valley erupted with the rifle fire. Above the crackling of the burning forest Peter could hear no sound. But he saw the little puffs of smoke and the Indians drop in mid-stride. The blazing woods created a wind of their own, a hot and terrible wind which swept through the trees. The flames leaped and darted down the sides of the valley and swept over the village. The Maclaren touched Peter on the shoulder and the horrified boy arose. They ran off up the mountain, pell mell, the hot breath of the flames following them, the report of exploding and crashing trees ringing in their ears.

On the mountain tops the trees thinned out to be replaced by scrub and rocks. Here the mountain men gathered to look down at the yellow and red cauldron which they had created below.

Peter was white with the horror of the deed. Not even the thought of the little girl, lying dead in the black dust with the rag doll a few feet away, could justify the deed in his mind. But the men of the mountains showed neither pleasure nor pity. They watched the inferno they had created through somber eyes and then went back to their homes.

There had been a massacre of their kind, and they had revenged it by another massacre. It was the law as they saw it and any other course on their part would have been unnatural.

Chapter 14

PETER STAYED four years in all in the mountains with the Maclaren of Spey. He had been a boy of eleven when the Maclaren had found him on the beach and decided that he might be worth saving. He was fifteen when the incident occurred which resulted in his leaving. In that time he had grown nearly a foot and a half. By fifteen Peter Treegate was but an inch short of six feet and still growing. His chest was big and his muscles were tough, lithe and strong. His face was tanned the color of a leather glove and his hair hung down over his shoulders. He could outwrestle the Maclaren of Spey and once when the Maclaren had broken a leg, he carried him on his back a journey of thirty miles over the mountains, back to their shack.

The Maclaren after that had paid him a great compliment. "Lad," he said between clenched teeth when Peter got him to the shack, "ye're almost as good as Jamie." Jamie was one of the Maclaren's sons, long dead at Culloden.

Many things changed in the world in those four years. In London a king had, by bribery, threats and diplomatic stealth, taken into his own hands the government of his country, hoodwinking, through his personally appointed ministers, a parliament which was for the most part too corrupt to care.

Gentlemen with large country estates were elected unopposed to this parliament for no other reason than that they owned large country estates. And many of these gentlemen, being required to vote upon some measure, first assured themselves who would pay the most money and cast their votes accordingly.

In Boston a mob of unemployed, joined by a further mob of angry merchants, had dressed themselves as Indians and, with wood ash on their faces, tipped several cargoes of tea into Boston harbor to protest against a monopoly on tea being given to the London East India Company. In New York a similar mob, calling themselves the Mohawks, had followed suit. And tea ships which reached Philadelphia were finally allowed to unload their cargoes in a warehouse where they rotted.

All over the thirteen colonies rebellion smoldered. The mobs of New York, Boston and Philadelphia found a counterpart in the countryside. Here there were not mobs but militia—militia who came from the field at the end of their day's work and executed clumsy maneuvers with clumsy rifles on the green before the nearest tavern.

Some of those in the militia were men in their fifties, and had memories of other militia drills during the French and Indian Wars. They told stories of those wars when the drilling was over and claimed that at many a battle the Redcoats had been saved only by the colonial militia. This militia trained in Vermont and New Hampshire, in Rhode Island and Massachusetts Bay Colony, in the Hampshire Grants and on down the coast to the Carolinas and Georgia.

The militia were answered by more Redcoats who poured into Boston and the port was sealed off by the British fleet. Boston, said the King in London through his minister Lord North, was to be brought to its knees. Not as much as a fishing vessel was to be allowed to come in or go out of its harbor and, since Boston was a port and lived as a port, it was plain that Boston must submit to the King's law or die.

But Boston didn't die. Carters from as far away as Pennsylvania and New York and even the Carolinas drove their wagons to Boston, bringing the grain, timber and leather and the clothing Boston needed for life. And in Philadelphia a congress of representatives met and solemnly proclaimed an embargo of the mother country. After December, 1774, they decided, no cargo would leave any American port for any English port.

These developments had their effect even in the Carolina mountains, for more and more people were pushing their way from the coast inland. The good coastal lands were now owned and the new settlers looked for virgin country and they trickled over the hills and then into the mountains. Settlers built shacks in the valley beyond and the Maclaren of Spey pondered this development for a long while. Often he would go alone to the mountain divide, from which he could look down into the valley and stare for hours at these shacks. And when he returned, he would say nothing for two or three days.

Then one day he made up his mind. "We maun burn them oot," he said to Peter.

"Why?" the boy asked.

"They've no right here," said the highlander. "This all belongs to the Maclaren o' Spey."

"They're not in your valley," Peter replied.

"They will be afore long," said the Maclaren.

"We can talk to them," Peter said. But the Maclaren would do no such thing. It was beyond his dignity to call upon a stranger. Since he was a chieftain, it was the strangers' duty, whoever they were, to call upon him and ask permission to put up their shacks.

Peter decided to talk to the strangers himself. He didn't tell the Maclaren, fearing he might be forbidden, but went off one morning, climbed the ridge of the mountain, and by midafternoon was near the two shacks.

Now he appeared cautiously, spying on the land, moving quietly from tree to tree. He found that there were five men in the shacks. There was a river which flowed swiftly through this valley and the men had built their shacks close to the river. They were sitting outside and eating a dinner out of a iron pot which formed a common dish. They had big-bladed axes by them. Peter stepped suddenly into the open, his rifle in the crook of his arm. He did not make a sound but he knew that the sudden movement would attract the men. They stopped eating and looked around at him, astonished.

They saw what they took to be a tall and extremely broad-shouldered Indian clad in deerskin, his hair almost down to his waist, and carrying a rifle. They looked fearfully at one another and got slowly to their feet.

Peter smiled in gentle reproof. "I could have killed two of you easy," he said. "You don't belong in the mountains. Where are you from?"

There was a sigh of relief from the group and one man said, "Charlestown," and he jerked his head to indicate the direction of the city.

"What are you doing here?"

"Cutting trees."

"Why?"

"Need the lumber."

Peter looked at the two shacks. They were completely built and he saw no reason for cutting further trees. The men saw him glance at the cabins and, understanding the reason for the look, one of them said, "Lumber fetches a good price in Charlestown. We plan to float it down this river, come spring when the floods are here . . ."

But something connected with the use of trees was stirring in Peter's mind, something long forgotten. A long, long time ago someone had told him that trees were valuable. Someone had told him how to select a good tree for boards. Who was this someone? It was someone with a sharp, impatient voice—an old man. And he had kept his lumber in a place he called "the forest."

"What do you use the trees for?" Peter asked and he could feel the sweat breaking out on the palms of his hands and on his neck.

"For ships . . ."

Ships. He knew about ships. He'd come off a ship which had been wrecked. But ships had nothing to do with the angry man who kept his lumber in a place he called the forest.

"What else . . . ?"

"Tables. Chairs. Carts. All kinds of things. Barrel staves . . ."

Barrel staves! That was it. That was the angry little man's use for the lumber. There was a boy—was it himself?—and the angry man was to teach him how to make barrel staves. He had called him one day and asked him to bring him a shaving of pine and one of fir and one of cedar. And then he had asked this boy to tell him, by the shaving, when had been the rainy years and when the dry years during the lifetime of the tree.

But who was this boy and who was this man? He tried to think of the man's name. It was a name something like a tree. Tree . . . something. He couldn't think of it. The boy then. What was the boy's name? That had had something to do with a tree too. He could feel himself trembling. The boy's name was . . . was . . . Peter! Yes. Peter! The same name as his. It was Peter Tree something.

Suddenly he shouted, "Peter Treegate! Peter Treegate! That's who I am! And the man was Treaser!" And without further explanation he turned and dashed back into the forest, running up the slope of the mountain, leaving the five men gaping at each other.

He did not stop until he had reached the shack and all the time he ran memories were exploding in his mind like flashes of lightning on a summer's night.

"I know who I am," he shouted to the Maclaren as he flung through the door. "I'm Peter Treegate. I lived in Boston. I have a father in Boston and a brother in Philadelphia. And a man called Blake killed someone on the Long Wharf. That's how I got on the ship. I know the ship now. It was the *Maid of Malden* . . ." He tumbled the story out in a torrent of words, the phrases ripped, as it were, from his brain. And when he had done, he sat on his cot and stared at the Maclaren as if he were seeing him for the first time.

"Talk more, boy," said the Maclaren. "Talk on. Root it out, and ye'll be rid o' the black curse that has been on ye. Were ye ever in Scotland? Do ye know aught of a massacre? Ye've cried out 'Massacre' in yer sleep many a night."

"Massacre," said Peter. "The Boston Massacre. The

Redcoats fired into the crowd and people screamed and fell down. The blood looked black in the snow." And suddenly he knew what it was about the Thomastown massacre that had stirred his mind so uneasily. He poured the whole story out, repeating parts of it time and again until he had it all clear and in all this time the Maclaren said nothing.

When he had finished, the Maclaren got up and went out of the shack. He did not return that night or the next day and in the interval Peter went over his own story time and again, getting more and more details so that he remembered such people as Sam Adams and Governor Hutchinson and Goldie, his fellow apprentice. But most of all, he thought about his father who had gone to London and who had a musket over the fireplace of his house in Boston which he had carried at the battle of the Plains of Abraham.

He examined his feeling toward his father and found, to his surprise, that he felt cold toward him. He felt, indeed, something more than cold. He felt hostile and, when he tried to discover why, for he remembered that at one time he had loved his father, he concluded that it was because he had been deserted. His father had given him to Mr. Fielding—the name came quite readily to his mind—as an apprentice and had gone away to London. He had left him alone and all the terrors of his life had stemmed from that desertion.

Then he thought of the Maclaren of Spey. He loved the savage Highlander. Not a word of affection had ever passed between them. But for his own father he felt nothing but coldness and hostility.

What about his brother?

He could remember him only vaguely. But he felt a glow of affection at the thought of a brother, who he decided must now be about nine years of age.

The Maclaren stayed away two nights and a day. When he returned, about noon of the second day, he said nothing, but he looked infinitely weary. The bone of his broken leg had been set only roughly, and Peter knew that when the Maclaren was tired he limped. He limped now.

Peter heated up a stew of deer meat and gave some to the Maclaren. But the Scotsman ate only a little and then got into his cot and went to sleep.

He stayed in bed two days, still not talking, and Peter thought he must have taken a fever and hung around, trying to minister to him. He had picked up the highlander's habit of silence and spent his time with his thoughts.

The third morning after his return, the Maclaren got up from his cot and turned on Peter savagely.

"Ye've no need tae stay," he said. "Ye may go tae yer faither in Boston toon and I'll stay here in the mountains. I wouldna' give ye another thought when I saw the last of yer back through the trees. I dinna want ya hanging aroond oot a pity for me. I'm a man has lived alone twenty-five years and more and can live alone another twenty-five wi'oot the company of a Sassenach whelp."

It astonished Peter that this was what had been bothering the Maclaren. The savagery of the words stung him, and he was hurt to the quick that the man would think he would leave him.

"I'll go if ye want me to," he said and picked up his rifle and went out of the shack. He went up to the top of the mountain but his heart grew heavier with every step and when he got there he turned and came back.

"Mon," said the Maclaren as he re-entered the shack. "Ye've no resolution. Yer like a woman for changing yer mind." But there were tears in the highlander's eyes and they fell down his cheeks and along the white scars left by the bear's claws.

"You want me back?" said Peter for, despite the tears, he did not want to seem to surrender too easily.

"Och boy," said the Maclaren, "ye're bluid and bone of my own. I carried ye here from the sea and ye carried me on yer own back a wee step. I showed ye how to use a gun and how tae fight. I dinna sire ye but I made a man oot of ye." He grabbed Peter by the shoulders and looked straight in his face.

"If ye'd crossed the mountain," he said, "I'd hae killed myself." And then he seized the boy and hugged him like a bear and put back his head and laughed a great laugh of joy, and said that the Maclarens would live again for the clan was reborn.

After that, the two were closer together than they had ever been before. The Maclaren talked of moving farther to the west, for he did not like the strangers in the other valley. Peter said he was willing to go with him, and indeed he would have gone anywhere the Scotsman suggested.

But, deep inside, he was conscious of other ties. There was his brother in Philadelphia—a vague memory. But he would not want his brother to think that he had been deserted as he felt that his father had deserted him.

The thought of his father kept returning. His father's name was John. He had been, it seemed to Peter, a big man. He had also been a stern man, but capable of strange little kindnesses. Peter could remember one time his father had been especially kind to him for a week and during that week seemed very sad at the same time. He decided that must have been the week when his mother had died, though he could not remember his mother. When he thought of his father like this, the desertion he attributed to him became blurred. His father had had to go to England. Maybe he didn't want to go. And certainly he must wonder what had become of his son.

Peter tried to shrug these thoughts out of his mind and concentrate all his affection on the Maclaren. But much as he loved the Maclaren, his father's image kept recurring to him, and sometimes he dreamed that his father was looking for him and calling his name.

For three months he continued in this state, and the Scotsman noted that the boy was becoming increasingly moody. He would turn on him harshly and tell him to stop his mooning and perform some task.

Then one day, when they were both sitting outside the shack, silent together, the Maclaren suddenly went inside and returned with his gun and powder horn.

"Get yer gun," he said, "and come with me."

"Where are we going?" Peter asked, for they had a good supply of meat, so hunting was unnecessary.

"Tae Boston toon," said the Maclaren. "Tae see yer faither. I'm thinking it must be close on a thousand miles and the snows are due."

Chapter 15

THE CITY OF Boston, when it thought of John Treegate, thought of him with respect and with pity. He was, and had been for many years, a prominent member of that mixed and turbulent community. He was a friend of the governor as he was a friend of John Adams, who had shocked many in Boston by defending the very soldiers who had fired into the crowd before the Old State House many years before. He was an outspoken man and a man of rigid views and his views were directly opposed to the growing sentiment of the city. They were that the people of Boston were subjects of the King, and should obey the King's laws. If these laws were found oppressive, then the remedy lay in presenting the case for the colonies to the ministry in London. There was and never would be any justification for violence—for mob rule.

Mr. Benjamin Franklin of Philadelphia held this view. John Treegate had conferred with him often in London during his mission there—a mission undertaken to plead with Lord North for a relaxation of the restriction on manufacturers in the thirteen American colonies. On that mission he had sat some several months in Lord North's waiting room surrounded by the elegant peacock gentlemen who were also waiting on His Lordship. The mission had ended in the shattering news of the death of his son and he had returned to Boston.

It was on John Treegate's return that the town started to pity the man. He had changed and for the worst. His temper was shorter and his tolerance, never a strong point with a man of such clearcut views, was altogether gone. He denounced the Boston Tea Party, when the East India Company tea had been flung into the harbor, as a piece of vandalism and mob rule and wanton destruction of property unparalleled in modern times. He called on John Hancock, having heard that he was one of the "Indians" involved in the adventure, and denounced him in the rudest terms in John Hancock's own spacious drawing room. He quarreled with his old friend Mr. Fielding to whom he had apprenticed his son for, though he would not admit it and maintained the quarrel arose from the wide differences in their political views, secretly he blamed the man for the loss of his son.

He quarreled, indeed, with everyone and became more and more a lonely figure in the town. Each thirteenth of September, he continued to give a dinner to commemorate the glorious battle of the Plains of Abraham when the French had been driven from the American continent which would now be forever British. But as the years went by, fewer and fewer accepted his invitation. Most of his old comrades sent their regrets—they had to be away on business that day, or they were ill and could not come, or they were recovering from an illness but confined still to their homes.

And when September 13, 1774, rolled around, John Treegate sat alone in his dining room before a table laid for twelve, for not one of his old comrades was able to join him in a toast to the King's health and the continued prosperity and expansion of the British Empire.

He then sent his servant around to the British garrison and invited the officers to join him. The notice was short enough but invitations to Redcoat officers were rare and eight gentlemen presented themselves in regimentals, coming in ones and twos.

With these, instead of his old American comrades, John Treegate drank the King's health and talked of the great battle. The officers listened politely, one or two of them even with interest. John Treegate showed the gentlemen the musket he had carried on that day, still in its rack over his fireplace.

One of the officers, a Major Pitcairn of the Royal Marines, asked permission to examine the piece, but Mr. Treegate refused the permission gently but firmly. "I have made a vow, gentlemen," he said, "that I would never take that musket down again unless for the defense of my country."

The musket was toasted, the great and glorious day of September 13th was toasted, the colonial militia was toasted and the regular army was toasted. And then the gentlemen made their adieus and went back to their barracks, leaving John Treegate alone in his empty house, and the loneliness was crushing.

Any other citizen of Boston who had thus openly entertained the Redcoat officers would have had his house mobbed on the following day. His business premises would likely also have been mobbed and life made so uncomfortable for him that he would, without a doubt, have left for Halifax, Nova Scotia, where loyalty to the King ran high.

But not John Treegate. Even Sam Adams was prepared to

admit that John Treegate's convictions, though unpopular, were honest. They were not based, as were the politics of many Tories, on hopes of personal profit. They were based upon a principle, the principle of the loyalty of the subject to the King, and the rooted belief that the King sought only the good of his subjects and was their protection.

So Sam Adams, still scurrying around from tavern to town meeting, from mean hovels near the docks to the graceful quarters of the wealthier citizens, passed the word that John Treegate was not to suffer any hardship or affront. And so he was left unmolested. He was an honorable man and in the loss of his son he had suffered heavily. The town tolerated him but left him alone. And the loneliness ate deeper and deeper into the man, and drove him more and more to seek the company of the British garrison.

Then, one January day in 1775, John Treegate's son returned. To the astonishment of the people of Boston, who were not easily astonished in those days, two wild-looking men clad in buckskins, and with cloaks of goat skin flung over their shoulders to protect them from the wind and snow, padded into the city over the Roxbury neck. They did not walk with the short inefficient steps of townsmen, but with the long lope, the leg swung easily from the hips, that was the walk of mountain people. They carried big hunting knives in their belts in scabbards of hide and powder horns and bullet bags on bandoliers slung over their shoulders. But they had no rifles. Their rifles they had left, on advice, at a tavern in Roxbury village. No one was allowed to come into Boston carrying firearms.

As it was, this savage-looking pair had trouble with the patrol of Welsh troops who guarded the Roxbury peninsula. A Redcoat had tried to take their knives and, unable to persuade these two to part with them, had called his officer. The officer, uncomfortable in the presence of a little crowd of loafers which quickly gathered, backed up his men and demanded that the knives be handed over.

Then the shorter of these two men had said in a thick Scotch accent, "The only way ye can ha' it, mon, is in yer heart." He had drawn his knife so quickly that it fairly seemed to leap into his hand. And he said the words so coolly that it was plain he meant them, and that the death of this particular officer would be but an incident, and a small incident, in the life of this man.

"Who are you?" the officer demanded.

"I'm the Maclaren o' Spey," said the other and he shucked off his goatskin cloak to show a rag of tartan and a beautiful silver broach which fastened it to his buckskins. Then he added, coldly, "I maybe cut your faither's throat at Drummossie Muir which you Sassenachs call Culloden."

"And you?" said the officer to the other, who was several inches taller than his companion, though much younger.

"Peter Treegate."

"Peter Treegate?"

"Yes."

"Any relation of Mr. John Treegate?"

"His son."

There was a little buzz in the crowd. The officer looked hard at the younger and the taller of the two, turned to the soldier and said, "Let them pass." He would have given a month's pay to be at John Treegate's house when his son returned. He had been there last September and had heard briefly of this son who had disappeared and was believed murdered. There was another son somewhere in Philadelphia but this couldn't be the one. The other son's name was Stephen.

And so the Maclaren of Spey and Peter Treegate, after a journey of over a thousand miles, much of it across mountains and through wilderness and in the dead of winter, walked into Boston.

Not even the ancient foreman Mr. Treaser, in his remarkable journey up the Strand in London, clad in a mourning suit made for the death of Queen Anne, caused a greater sensation.

Boston was full of idlers. There was no work to be had of any sort. With the closing of the port, the business of the city had ceased and it now lived on the charity of other cities. And the idlers saw the strange couple and followed them in a mob, shouting questions which the two ignored. Through the mob sped the word that John Treegate's son was back—back from the dead. Several detached themselves from the mob and sped into the house of John Treegate to tell him the news. And one of those who did this was Sam Adams.

Peter and the Maclaren of Spey did not go immediately to Mr. Treegate's house. The boy was nervous over the reunion with his father and sought, now that the long journey was over, to delay the moment. He had wondered many times what he would say when he met his father—the man who he still felt had deserted him as a child. And so the two went first instead to a place for which Peter had, curiously enough, a warmer feeling. They went to the home of Mr. Fielding.

An outside railing prevented the mob following them to the door, which was opened by a rag of a woman, with stringy hair and a stringy face, whom Peter recognized as the servant Agatha.

She immediately threw her apron over her face and ran screaming into the house, yelling that the Indians were attacking the city and two of them, at that moment, ready to slaughter the occupants of Mr. Fielding's home.

This brought out the tall figure of Mrs. Fielding, who arrived with her head still cocked to one side listening, as she always listened, to the voices of the "other world." She looked sharply for a second at the Maclaren of Spey and pointed a long bony finger at him dramatically and said, "You are a believer. I know it." The Maclaren immediately crossed himself and fumbled in a little bag which he kept on his belt. He hurriedly took out of this a pinch of powdered root and threw it on the ground, this being an infallible method of getting rid of hags and other evil beings.

But Mrs. Fielding did not disappear. Instead she turned to Peter and said, "I knew you were not dead, Peter Treegate. I called to you many times and you were not in the other world. But I saw you once lying on a wild seacoast." And then she added surprisingly, "You have grown a great deal. You must have drunk a lot of potato soup. It is very good for boys."

Mr. Fielding was in his office—the little room with a door giving out on "the forest"—and the two went there to him. The cooper was busy writing at a small table. He looked around severely at the interruption and the goose quill fell from his hand, making a black blot on the sheet of white paper.

He got up from his chair and, staring at Peter, said, "Boy . . . boy . . ." And then he sat down again, shaking and white.

"It's all right, Mr. Fielding," said Peter. "It's me and alive."

"Have you seen your father?" asked Mr. Fielding when he had got some control over himself.

"No," said Peter. "Not yet."

"Then go to him, for the love of God," said Mr. Fielding. "His heart is dead inside of him, for he has lived alone and with grief too long. You will find him terribly changed, Peter . . . a stranger to you, no doubt. You must be patient with him. He has grown apart from all his old friends. Yet, with you back, and with your love, all that will surely alter."

"I am not sure that I can give him love," said Peter slowly. "He left me here as a child to go to England, as he would have left a piece of furniture . . ."

"Oh, you do not understand, Peter," cried Mr. Fielding. "He felt it was his duty to go—to secure some relaxation of the laws. He felt it was his duty to the colonies and to the King. Duty has always come first with your father."

"Then he must not complain," said Peter grimly, "if love comes not at all."

"My dear boy," said Mr. Fielding, taking Peter's hands and speaking very earnestly, "do not judge him harshly. He lost his wife, your good mother. Then he lost his son. He is about to lose his world, the British world and obedience to the King, which he holds should always remain here. It will not remain. It is going daily, and the shock of that, without your help, will shatter him completely. Remember that and go to him now."

He almost pushed Peter through the door. The boy went out, followed by the Maclaren. The mob was still outside, but now it was a quiet mob, and Peter recognized standing by the gate the untidy and yet strangely commanding figure of Sam Adams.

"I thought it better to tell your father that you had returned, Mr. Treegate," he said. "He is expecting you."

Peter looked at him, slightly angry. "You are no friend of

my father's that I recall," he said. "I have heard him say that you should be hanged."

Sam Adams shook his head. "Your father, young sir," he said, "does not know who his friends are. Yet often the worthiest of men are the last to join a cause."

Peter went through the gate and noted that now none of the mob followed them. Sam Adams again, he thought. Sam Adams, the king of the beggars.

He reached his father's house and it looked strangely small to him. He stood before the door looking at the knocker which, the last time he had seen it, had been well beyond his reach. Now it was level with his shoulders. He looked at the Maclaren and the Scotsman's face was as hard as rimrock, the white scars made by the bear's claws showing like lines of frost against his tanned cheek.

"Knock and be damned tae it," said the Maclaren.

But Peter could not knock. His stomach was a pit of anxiety. His hand trembled and fell short of the knocker.

The Scotsman swore at him and said savagely, "Ye've turned woman on me. By Rab, I'll knock on the door o' hell itself." With that he reached for the knocker and slammed it hard three times on its brass base.

The sound thundered through the house and when it died away they heard footsteps coming downstairs and along a hallway—firm, unhurried footsteps.

Then the door opened and father and son faced each other.

They stood silent for a moment, seeing but not believing.

And then John Treegate threw his arms around his son and cried "Peter" in a strangled voice and dragged him into the house.

Chapter 16

PETER TREEGATE stayed a little over four months in his father's house in Boston. They were months of harassment, strain and anxiety, for when the first swells of emotion had died down a coolness took their place.

It was hard for Peter, reflecting later, to decide exactly how this had come about. Certainly the Maclaren of Spey was not to be blamed. Or was he? The highlander stayed in John Treegate's house three days, refusing the bed put at his disposal and sleeping on the floor. Then he could stand it no more. The walls were like coffin walls to him. The furniture, with its brocaded upholstery, filled him with a scorn which was based upon fear and distrust of such chattels. The night before he left, he quarreled violently with Peter's father.

The quarrel was inevitable. Two men could not share one son. But it did not erupt over Peter, but over the Scotsman's reminiscences of the Battle of Culloden.

He gave some details of this battle one day at dinner, and spoke with relish over the number of Redcoats who had been slain, and with passion of the butchery of the Duke of Cumberland which had followed and in which his whole clan had been wiped out.

Mr. Treegate agreed that the cruelty was excessive, but added incautiously that, at the time, the Scottish clans were rebels and rebels must be dealt with harshly.

The Maclaren was on his feet in a second, flaming with rage. "Do ye think yer God, mon," he cried, "tae decide who is ruler and who rebel? Do ye think the clans o' Scotland ha' no right tae rule theirselves, as they had done a thousand years before the Sassenaches came over the border? Yer clane daft! A mon's a mon and hae his rights, and I was as great a mon and a better chieftain in my time than yer fat Georgie on his throne in London toon wi' his Redcoats pushing their muskets in the face o' the people tae keep him there."

With that he flung out of the room, and the next morning he had gone. He sent a messenger around later in the day to say that he was staying at Sam Adams' house. Peter knew the significance of this. The Maclaren of Spey, staying in the home of the man he judged the enemy of John Treegate, had thrown down the gauntlet in his own fashion. Stung by John Treegate's reference to the "rebels" at Culloden, he had in defiance joined the rebels of Boston. And Peter learned a week later that Mr. Adams had obtained a commission as captain for the Maclaren of Spey in the Massachusetts militia—itself an enormous tribute to the influence of Sam Adams, for the Massachusetts militia was very touchy at receiving as a captain a man who knew nothing of the colony and, furthermore, cursed all the members of the militia as Sassenaches.

But he knew how to fight and to use a rifle and to take cover and he made a good captain.

When the Scotsman had gone, it eased matters in some ways between Peter and his father. But, in other ways, his absence made their relationship far more difficult.

Peter would have followed the highlander, but that he sensed his father's enormous need for him. He believed that if he left, his father would not have survived the shock. So he stayed. And because, in staying, he was choosing between the Maclaren and his father, he resented his father the more. Yet it could not be denied that, with the Scotsman out of the house, the two could talk more intimately. This they did, cautiously at first, trying to break down the years that lay between them, and not hurt each other's feelings unduly. And then the caution went and their discussions became frank. With the frankness came resentment and anger.

One day Peter got out what had lain long unspoken in his mind—the conviction that his father had not cared greatly for him as a boy and had left him among strangers to go on his business to London.

Mr. Treegate blanched when Peter blurted out the charge and for some time was so overcome by shock that he could not reply.

When he did, it was in fumbling phrases and sentences, in which the word "duty" occurred and recurred.

"Duty," cried Peter at length. "Duty to whom? To me and my brother? Or to your own business?"

"To the people of these colonies," said Mr. Treegate quietly. "To my neighbors and to their King—your King and my King and their King—in England. Men may not so order their affairs that they may put their families before everything. Were such a view widely taken, government would be impossible and patriotism a jest."

He turned away from his son now and faced the fireplace as if he were ashamed of what he was about to add; ashamed that he might show some weakness which he did not wish his son to see.

"God, before whom I must one day stand for judgment, is my witness that I love you," he said. Then he added, to the fireplace, "It has not been easy being alone."

Peter went to him, took him by the shoulders and turned him gently around. "Forgive me," he said. "I didn't understand." And from that day there was no coldness or resentment between them, on that score.

But on the question of where their respective duties lay now, father and son could not see eye to eye. Mr. Treegate would not be shaken from his abhorrence of rebellion against the King and the King's government.

"Even if I could countenance it for a minute," he said, "with what is the rule of our sovereign lord the King to be replaced? With the rule of a mob led by Sam Adams? Is the wealth and the property of a nation, its prosperity and its future to be turned over to the hands of people who have not a penny in the world, not as much as a chair to their names and therefore no sense of responsibility? What is the goal of such people? I will tell you very simply. It is to destroy the nation for their own ends. It is not to build but to tear down. It is to replace government by anarchy and make loyalty a vice and rebellion a virtue."

"But what of this mob?" Peter asked. "Have they no rights? Must they always be propertyless and poor, dependent for their bread upon some act of parliament passed without reference to them. Why are there mobs—hungry people without work? They were not born to the mob, these people. They are condemned to it by the government which should be ruling in their behalf."

Mr. Treegate frowned for his son had touched upon a point to which he had no answer.

"A wise and just government looks after all its citizens," he said. "The King is the protector of his people."

"Then the government is not wise nor the King just," replied Peter, "for I traveled here a thousand miles and everywhere found men suffering from laws which they had no say in the making. And this city is garrisoned now as if for war. The port is closed. Thousands are idle . . . Is this protection?"

"It is the fruit of rebellion," said Mr. Treegate.

"Yes," said Peter bitterly. "We just bow our heads and be thankful to be abused. If we stand up like men and demand our rights, then comes what you call the fruit of rebellion—Cumberland the Butcher at Culloden, or General Gage starving out Boston."

"There is no butchery here," flared Mr. Treegate.

"No," said Peter. "Nothing but the butchery of rights which seem to me natural to every man."

After this exchange the two lived together in a state of torture, hurting each other by their presence, yet Peter was afraid of inflicting a greater and mortal hurt if he left. And all the time Peter went around Boston and saw the soldiers parading with fife and drum through the streets, and the hungry, sullen people watching this. He noted that in the Boston churches a soldier not infrequently sat at the foot of the pulpit, if a fiery sermon was expected, with a pistol in his hand, or toying with a bayonet, acting the complete uniformed bully. He spoke a great deal with Sam Adams, who seemed to be in and out of the city as often as a bird. And he spoke with Mr. Fielding and sometimes with old Mr. Treaser who, with no barrel staves to be made now, still reported each day for work to be with his beloved wood.

Soon he was returning to his father's house only for

dinner, and often he elected to take dinner alone rather than join the one or two British officers whom Mr. Treegate had stubbornly invited to dine with him.

A couple of times Peter, in the study of his father's house, glanced up at John Treegate's musket over the fireplace. Once he had loved it. Now he came to hate it. It was much the same musket as the Redcoats carried. And for Peter, it symbolized much the same thing as the Redcoats. Tyranny.

When the end of this unhappy state arrived, it came in one rocketing hour. For a whole night the city had been full of rumors of a big raid being made by the Redcoats in the direction of Lexington, with the object of seizing some arms and powder and the special purpose of seizing the persons of Sam Adams and John Hancock. Then the next day came stories of the militia firing on the Redcoats, and finally the Redcoats returned, carrying their bleeding wounded with them, but in a rout.

John Treegate went immediately to the British headquarters to ascertain what had happened and he returned white and shaken and looking very old. The awfulness of the news broke the strain which existed between himself and his son and he flung it on the boy who was seated in his study.

"It's war," he said. "The troops, about seven hundred of them, marched during the night to Lexington and Concord and fired on the militia on Lexington Green. Several were killed. In retaliation, the militia followed the line of march, firing at the soldiers right to the outskirts of Boston, killing scores—some say hundreds."

He strode up and down the room, his hands behind his back, and in a state of the greatest agitation.

"It is too late now for protest," he broke out. "Too late for meetings and conciliations. I have been loyal to my King and my country to this very moment. I have sought by every means to conciliate and to quieten matters down. I have not agreed with much that has been done here in Boston and I still do not agree with it."

Anger flooded into his face so swift and strong that Peter saw the veins stand out on his father's forehead and his eyes blaze as he had never seen them blaze before.

"My King!" he shouted. "My country! For the two of them I fought before you were born. But I will support no King and no country which marches armed troops to the number of seven hundred through a peaceful countryside at night to seize two men. I will support no rule by colonels and no government by musket. Where soldiers protect the peaceful citizen, they are worthy of support. When a King protects his subjects, he shall have my loyalty. But when soldiers become the King's form of government and march against the citizenry they are to cherish, then I am no longer a loyal subject of such a king.

"Boy," he said, stopping directly in front of Peter, "have you a gun?"

"Yes," said Peter.

"And I also have one," said his father.

He looked up over the fireplace at his musket. "I had never expected to be doing this," he said. He hesitated and then took the weapon down swiftly. He examined the flint and the pan.

"I do not know how we are to get out of Boston armed," he said. "But I will shoot my way out if need be." And he led the way out of the room.

On the top of Breed's Hill outside Boston, several hundred men waited in hastily dug earthworks and they waited for the most part in silence. The sun was hot and the air still and before them, down the slope, the long grass was ready for cutting for the hay crop. There were a few red poppies in the grass and some cornflowers, and from it came the shrill chirping of insects.

Over the top of the grass the men could see, lining the bottom of the hill, where the waters lapped the shore, platoon after platoon of red-coated infantry. They had been coming ashore from barges all morning and were in full battle dress. They formed in line upon line, their bayonets glittering in the pleasant summer air.

Among the men on the top of the hill were John Treegate, his son Peter and a dark savage Scotsman who styled himself the Maclaren of Spey. And not far away from these was an elderly cabinetmaker called Treaser and a hundred yards further, unknown to these, a boy of seventeen who answered to the name of Goldie, who had come up only the night before from Delaware, where he had a small boatmaker's yard on the Chesapeake.

Among the men at the bottom of the hill, in lines as straight and as red as a poker, were many in splendid regimentals who had been equally splendidly dressed in the height of civilian fashion in London only a few years previously. Then they had been waiting, as it were, for nothing in the waiting room of Lord North.

Now the nothing had come to something. They found themselves, to their amusement and surprise, with lucrative army commissions in their pockets and the task of sweeping some farmers off the top of a hill in far away Massachusetts Bay Colony.

Among the soldiers they commanded was a man who had

for many years removed and replaced a chain which guarded the entrance to Puddinghouse Lane in London and two others who had carried a strange figure dressed in Queen Anne mourning around the city in a sedan chair.

There was a soldier who had for a shilling cleaned up the rubbish in the yard of Mr. Fielding, a cooper of Boston. He did not know that Mr. Fielding was waiting for him, to give him another sort of payment at the top of the hill.

There were two other soldiers who had been branded upon the thumb for firing into the mob outside of the Old State House in Boston, and there was a soldier called Blake who said little of his past though he had joined the regiment in Boston and he was Boston born.

He had good reason for saying nothing of his past for his past included a murder. And the boy on whom he had hoped to blame the murder was in the earthworks at the top of the hill waiting for him.

The insects chirped, a skylark rose out of the grass and chattered on fluttering wings in the blue sky which matched the blue cornflowers. Then the drums below rolled and the fifes shrilled and the red lines moved off up the hill, their bayonets glittering before them.

The lines came nearer and nearer, the men grunting under the sweat of the climb, with their hundred-pound packs on their backs. The men on the hilltop heard their grunts and heard the swish of the long grass on their gaiters, and these small noises seemed to fill the whole world.

Then someone shouted, "Don't shoot until you see the whites of their eyes!"

John Treegate thought of the Redcoats at the Plains of Abraham and looked at his son. There were tears in his eyes but he raised his musket and held it steady on the red line advancing toward him.

There was a shout of "Drummossie Muir!" from the Maclaren of Spey and then a roar from the muskets on the top of the hill, and the Redcoats disappeared in a cloud of thick smoke.

THE END OF THE BEGINNING

Afterword

History was always a favorite subject of mine, so that I read it avidly in school and have continued to do so since. It is the basic stuff of most of prose literature, for a novel, properly viewed, is but history brought down to an individual level, even though the work be entirely imaginary.

Now, most of the childhood and later reading I did of history concerned wars, and while the relation of the battles and campaigns was interesting, I found as I grew older a sort of void in them. Most of the wars seemed quite senseless—great conflicts over the acquisition of land or the right to thrones which, changing the destiny for a while of one country or another, were fought for position or possession, with no deeper purpose behind them.

All such wars told nothing of the men who fought in them and their families; why the soldiers faced the cannonade, and how their families and neighbors supported them and grieved over them or cheered them or opposed or denounced them as confounded fools. Love, fear, cowardice, courage, indecision—all the agonies of those involved were missing from the accounts of great campaigns.

When I came to the United States in the 1940s, I started really reading for the first time the history of the American Revolution. To be sure, I had learned of it in English schools, where the issue was quite straightforward. The misled British colonists in America, relieved at last of the threat of a French invasion from Canada by the glorious victory of General Wolfe at the Battle of Abraham Heights, had demanded their independence, and eventually gained it with the support of England's ancient enemy, France. That I think is a fair summary of the story as I got it, and it is amusing to reflect that deep down that is still often the British point of view. It is a sin, unforgivable, not to wish to be British, I assure you as an Irishman.

But reading the American account, I became more and more excited. Here was a war fought not for position or possession but for ideas, for ethical viewpoints; in essence, for the individual's right to be subject only to the laws which he himself had a hand in making. The most important war then, in my mind, in the history of Western man.

It was this slowly revealed view of the American Revolution that inspired me to write the book you now have in your hand. But I wanted also to show how this struggle for liberty, personal and national, affected one family—the Treegate family—and particularly Peter Treegate, whose father had worn the King's coat at that glorious Battle of Abraham Heights.

Here then is the result. Though fiction, I believe it reflects truth. Not all the truth, but some part of it. It is not a work of July 4th patriotism. What was fought for and achieved in that revolution belongs to all mankind, and so is far greater than any nation. But it was Americans who put the matter to battle-test, and that first shot not only was heard around the world but echoes around the world to this day.

LEONARD WIBBERLEY
Hermosa Beach, California November 1983

About the Author

Leonard Wibberley (1915-1983) was a prolific author and journalist. A father of six, he wrote over fifty books for children, some under the pseudonyms of Patrick O'Connor and Christopher Webb. His excellent historical fiction includes the seven volume Treegate series, which takes place during the Revolutionary War and the War of 1812. *John Treegate's Musket* opens this series with the events leading up to the War.

Part of Wibberley's success in writing for children is related in his own words: "Basically it is for the child inside myself that I write my children's books, for that child lives on into my more somber years." Like Stevenson and others of his favorite authors, Goldsmith, Milne, Lewis and Tolkien, Wibberley's main concentration in his stories is on the characters, from which he usually developed the plot. Using this method and liberally implementing his wry sense of humor, he produced his numerous works, ranging from fantasy to biography.

As an adult novelist, Wibberley is most remembered for *The Mouse That Roared*, an amusing satire about a duchy that defeats the United States with the long bow.

A native of Ireland, Leonard Wibberley lived in California for many years.

LIVING HISTORY LIBRARY

The Living History Library is a collection of works for children published by Bethlehem Books, comprising quality reprints of historical fiction and non-fiction, including biography. These books are chosen for their craftsmanship and for the intelligent insight they provide into the present, in light of events and personalities of the past.

TITLES IN THIS SERIES

Archimedes and the Door of Science, by Jeanne Bendick
Augustine Came to Kent, by Barbara Willard
Becky Landers, Frontier Warrior, by Constance L. Skinner
Beorn the Proud, by Madeleine Polland
Beowulf the Warrior, by Ian Serraillier
Big John's Secret, by Eleanore M. Jewett
Enemy Brothers, by Constance Savery
Galen and the Gateway to Medicine, by Jeanne Bendick
God King, by Joanne Williamson
The Hidden Treasure of Glaston, by Eleanore M. Jewett
Hittite Warrior, by Joanne Williamson
If All the Swords in England, by Barbara Willard
Jamberoo Road, by Eleanor Spence
John Treegate's Musket, by Leonard Wibberley
Madeleine Takes Command, by Ethel C. Brill
Nacar, the White Deer, by Elizabeth Borton de Treviño
The Mystery of the Periodic Table, by Benjamin D. Wiker
The Reb and the Redcoats, by Constance Savery
Red Falcons of Trémoine, by Hendry Peart
Red Hugh, Prince of Donegal, by Robert T. Reilly
Shadow Hawk, by Andre Norton
The Small War of Sergeant Donkey, by Maureen Daly
Son of Charlemagne, by Barbara Willard

Sun Slower, Sun Faster, by Meriol Trevor
The Switherby Pilgrims, by Eleanor Spence
Victory on the Walls, a Story of Nehemiah,
    by Frieda C. Hyman
The Wind Blows Free, by Loula Grace Erdman
The Winged Watchman, by Hilda van Stockum
Year of the Black Pony, by Walt Morey